HERE THERE BE HORRORS

HERE THERE BE HORRORS

PEGGY CHRISTIE

Dark Workings of Wild Women is published by Dragon's Roost Press.

This anthology is © 2025 Peggy Christie and Dragon's Roost Press.

Artwork by Sean Seal

Printed in the United States of America

Ingram ISBN: 978-1-956824-71-1

Print ISBN: 978-1-956824-69-8

Digital ISBN: 978-1-956824-67-4

Dragon's Roost Press

2470 Hunter Rd.

Brighton, MI 48114

thedragonsroost.biz

No AI was used in the creation of this book.

PUBLICATION HISTORY

"Find a Need" *Erie Tales II: Zombie Chronicles,* Great Lakes Association of Horror Writers (2009)
"Are We There Yet?" *Erie Tales III: Saturday Evening Ghost,* Great Lakes Association of Horror Writers (2010)
"On the Eighth Day He...Ooops" *Erie Tales IV: Tales of the Apocalypse/Tales of Resurrection Mary,* Great Lakes Association of Horror Writers (2011)
"From the World of Darkness" *Erie Tales VII: Myths and Mayhem,* Great Lakes Association of Horror Writers (2014)
"Brothers of Death" *Erie Tales VII: Holiday Horror,* Great Lakes Association of Horror Writers (2015)
"The Howling Wolf" *Erie Tales IX: Transformation,* Great Lakes Association of Horror Writers (2016)
"Hiding in Plain Sight" *Erie Tales X: Masquerade,* Great Lakes Association of Horror Writers (2017)
"Prodigal Son" *Erie Tales XI: Asylum,* Great Lakes Association of Horror Writers (2018)
"Red Rover" *Erie Tales XII: Little Bites and Finger Food,* Great Lakes Association of Horror Writers (2020)
"The 13th Man" *Erie Tales XIII: Unlucky Thirteen,* Great Lakes Association of Horror Writers (2020)

"Seep" *Erie Tales XIV: Secrets*, Great Lakes Association of Horror Writers (2022)

"The Dreadful Sisters Who Remain" *Erie Tales XV: It Came From The Movies*, Great Lakes Association of Horror Writers (2023)

To my fellow members and friends in GLAHW. From a humble beginning in 2007 to continued growth and evolution, thank you for believing in our group. And thank you for the inspiration you've given me in my writing journey.

CONTENTS

INTRODUCTION

For those who may not know, I belong to a horror writing group called the Great Lakes Association of Horror Writers. Or GLAHW for short. It started back in 2007 after another group I was in imploded, as is apt to happen when any large number of similar but differently minded people try to coexist. I, along with four other refugees from that group, started GLAHW.

Members have come and gone over the years but GLAHW is still powering forward. Every year we publish a themed anthology, Erie Tales, that is open to member submissions only. One of the criteria in our guidelines states that just because one is a member of the group, that does NOT automatically guarantee one will be published in the antho.

We like to give our members a chance but we're not going to accept just ANY story you throw at us. We like to keep our standards *relatively* high.

And I'm proud to say that I've had a story (sometimes two) published in every single Erie Tales anthology to date! That's seventeen anthologies so far (we did a small collection for 15½ before moving on to the full sized 16th anthology.) As of my writing this intro, Erie Tales Seventeen is in the editing phase. Hopefully, it'll be ready to go later this fall. And yes, I have a story in that one, too.

Four of my Erie Tales stories have already been published in one of my other collections, *Hell Hath No Fury.* But the ones you'll find in this book have not been released into the wild since their first publication adventures through Erie Tales, dating all the way back to 2008.

So enjoy reading about zombies, Japanese demons, shapeshifters, ghosts, and everything else that spilled out of my brain pan for GLAHW over the years. I'm sure you'll find something you like.

Peggy Christie

September, 2025

FIND A NEED AND FILL IT

"Mom! Dad! Got another one!" CJ called to his parents.

"Just throw it in the freezer with the rest," his father answered.

While CJ dragged the fresh catch to the basement freezer, his father continued to butcher the butt roasts from yesterday's hunting. He'd gotten a few steaks as well, but not as many as he'd hoped. Some days, the hunt brought great results, and sometimes just stringy bits of flesh. With the way the world was now, it wasn't all that surprising, but that didn't make it any less frustrating.

For the past eighteen months, the sun had been throwing beams of a new kind of radiation at the earth. No one could explain why or if it would ever stop. Even the most learned scientists in the world couldn't predict the strength or location of each incident. The levels changed every time, and they never occurred at regular intervals. But, wherever the radiation reached the Earth, the people...changed.

The dead began to walk. The living died from radiation poisoning and *then* walked. Not all were affected. Those who had died before embalming became common practice were not reanimated. The same was true for anyone who had been melted in acid, burned by fire, or had their muscle tissues destroyed in any way. It seemed reanimation required more than brain and bone. It needed flesh.

Once the reanimation began, it quickly spun out of control. Those who had escaped the sun's damage didn't always escape the walking dead. Their bites and scratches passed on the infection—for lack of a better word. Within hours of contamination, the once-living victim died and joined the ranks of the undead. It was like that old shampoo commercial. "I told two friends, and then they told two friends. And so on and so on and so on..." The dead multiplied out of control while the living dwindled.

Now, Karrie, her husband, Carl, and their son, CJ, were all that remained of Clawson, Michigan. Granted, it wasn't that big of a town to begin with, but eight thousand was better than three.

They weren't the only ones left in the world, though. At least, Karrie believed they weren't. She hoped they weren't. She prayed.

Karrie stepped up behind Carl and wrapped her arms around his waist. She gave him a quick squeeze and kiss on the shoulder. "What're you thinking about?"

"You know, the usual: The Super Bowl, taxes, what's happening on *NCIS*."

She slapped him on his behind and he snapped his fingers.

"Oh, right. Those things don't exist anymore. I forgot."

"Uh-huh. Where's CJ?"

"Downstairs." Carl jerked his thumb over his shoulder. "He brought in a new catch for the freezer."

"Another one? Wow, those traps you set are really working, huh?"

"Well, men *are* the hunters, you know. And women are the

gatherers. Why don't you go make yourself useful and gather me a sandwich?"

"If you weren't the only living man within a hundred-mile radius, I'd so leave your ass here and hook up with Jensen Ackles."

"Well, if you weren't the only woman, I'd hook up with uh...with uh...crap. What's the name of that actress from—?"

"Sarah Michelle Gellar?"

"No, no. She was in that comic book movie."

"*X-Men?*" Karrie offered.

"No, the other one."

"*The Hulk?*"

"No. *The Fantastic Four...?*" Carl rapped his knuckles against his forehead.

"Jessica Alba?"

"Yes! Thank you. Damn, that was going to keep me up all night if I couldn't think of her name."

"Ha! She'd never allow it. I'm going to see if CJ needs help."

"Okay, hon. Wait. What do you mean she'd never allow it?"

Karrie laughed as she headed downstairs, where she found CJ struggling with the freezer. The kid was tough for his age, but he was still only eight.

"Hey, peanut. Need some help?"

"Yeah, Mom. Thanks."

Karrie lifted the heavy lid of the chest freezer and propped it open with the built-in locking latch. She bent down and hefted the carcass into her arms. Dumping it into the freezer, she blew out a heavy breath.

"Whew! That was a heavy one. How on Earth did you get it down here by yourself?"

CJ flexed his biceps and grinned. He ran upstairs, yelling to his Dad about popsicles.

Smiling, Karrie bent down to clean up the trapping equipment CJ had dragged in with the carcass. She coiled up two lengths of rope and hung them on a hook by the freezer. One of the wooden stakes used to anchor the rope to the counterweight in the trap had splintered. She tossed it into a box reserved for firewood and made a mental note to talk to Carl about fashioning a new one. The blue plastic tarp lay open in the corner. Pools of blood filled the creases and folds. She'd deal with that once it dried.

CJ's hunting knife lay on the floor in a puddle of viscous looking blood. She grimaced as she grabbed some rubber gloves and a rag to clean it up. It was then she noticed several small dark red spots on the basement floor leading to the stairs. Beyond those were a few splats and short lines.

Karrie threw the gloves down and stormed upstairs.

"Young man! How many times have your father and I told you not to drip blood all over the house?"

Just as she reached the kitchen, a loud crack echoed outside. She stared at Carl. The shock on his face seemed to match her thoughts: Someone was shooting out there. Someone alive. Though the dead had reacquired their mobility this past year and a half, they had not regained their higher mental capacities or intricate motor skills.

CJ ran to the front window and peeked through a gap in the boards covering the glass. "It's Mr. Daniels. He's up on his roof!"

"Robert?" Carl asked. "He's still alive?"

"We haven't seen him since last Christmas. Where has he been?" Karrie wondered.

Carl ran to the hallway. "I'll ask him."

"We're coming with you!" Karrie shouted behind him.

He pulled down the retractable ladder, and Karrie and CJ followed Carl into the attic. From there, Karrie started up one of the three generators they had on hand to power whatever they needed in the house. Carl accessed the speaker system he'd wired in six months ago. He could broadcast and receive radio signals—as well as announce to the neighborhood the color, texture, and frequency of his bowel movements if he so desired. Back in the beginning, he'd used it religiously for a month as he tried to find survivors. But when no one responded, he shut it down and never touched it again. Until now.

"Rob? Rob! Is that you?"

Carl turned on the surveillance cameras and monitors he'd set up along with the broadcast radio. They could all see Rob on the third screen from the left. Carl flipped another switch to turn on the audio reception system so they could hear what was going on outside. Rob didn't say anything as he spun around as if trying to figure out where Carl's voice was coming from.

"Rob, it's Carl. Across the street, man."

Rob turned his attention on Carl's home. Understanding seemed to finally dawn on him and he waved in the general direction of the security cameras. Karrie smiled, happy to know their neighbor and friend was still alive.

She caught movement from the corner of her eye and turned to the monitor on the far right. A lone zombie shuffled its way down the street. Just as Karrie recognized the details of its fireman's uniform, she heard a loud crack. The back of the zombie's head exploded and it fell into the street. She looked back at the third monitor and watched Rob eject the spent cartridge from his rifle and then reload it.

She and Carl scanned the remaining monitors but saw no other zombies. More would be sure to show up since they were attracted to loud noises.

Carl clicked on the loudspeaker. "Rob! Hold up. I'm coming over."

Rob gave him a thumbs up before heading back inside his house. Within minutes, the two men stood in the street, shaking hands. Karrie and CJ watched the transaction from inside the attic.

"Rob, it's been months. We thought you were dead. Where've you been?"

"You know I've been prepping for something like this for years. So, I locked myself inside." Rob jerked his head toward his house. "I had enough provisions to last me a while, and I thought this would all blow over by the time I ran out. But, I guess my calculations were a bit off, huh?"

"What do you have left?"

"Not much," Rob replied. "A sleeve of Saltines, half a jar of peanut butter, a few bottles of water. I figured I'd just start shooting until I had one bullet left. Then..." His voice trailed off.

"Why didn't you just come to us?"

Rob shrugged. "Honestly, I didn't know anyone was still here. Those who survived got the hell out of town. There's no radio or TV anymore. My house is soundproofed and locked up tighter than a Scotsman's coin purse. I never heard anything or anyone. When I realized I was going to starve, I got on the roof. If I saw zombies shuffling around, I figured that meant it was still hell out here and I'd take out as many as I could."

"What if you didn't see any?" Carl asked.

"Well, I guess I'd start walking and see how far I'd get on a handful of peanut butter cracker sandwiches."

Carl raised an eyebrow at him.

Rob smiled. "Okay. Maybe I'd bust into a couple of homes, raid a few panty drawers, and *then* walk outta town."

"Rob, we have plenty to eat." Carl slapped him on the back and directed him over to his house. "Please come over. Karrie will be glad to know you're all right."

"Thanks, Carl."

Karrie and CJ made their way down to the living room and watched the two men through the front window. CJ darted off toward the front door but Karrie stopped him.

"CJ, you stay here."

"But, Mom," CJ whined.

"We don't know if it's completely clear yet. Wait. Here."

The boy pushed his glasses up on his nose and folded his arms in what had become his trademark posture of frustration. But he stayed inside while Karrie walked out the front door to greet her neighbor.

"Rob, it's so good to see you."

She threw her arms around him and gave him a big bear hug.

He pulled away, flushing pink in embarrassment. "Karrie, I told you before. Not in front of your husband."

She laughed and directed him to the front door. As he entered, CJ ran up to him. Rob held up his hand.

"CJ! High five."

The boy jumped up and slapped Rob's hand. CJ offered his own in return and Rob swiped it. CJ then grabbed Rob's arm and dragged him over to the couch.

"Rob! Where have you been? What happened to Roscoe and Dozer? Wanna see my hunting knife? Where's Annie? Have you killed any zombies? Wanna see my room?"

Before he could even consider answering the first question, let alone the following ones, Karrie shushed the boy.

"CJ. Give Rob a break. He just got here. We need to feed him first, okay?"

CJ slumped against the cushions, defeated.

Rob hooked his arm around the boy's neck and whispered in his ear, "Hey, while your Mom cooks dinner, you can show me your room. Cool?"

"All right!" CJ shouted.

The boy jumped up and dragged Rob by the hand.

"Roast is okay for dinner, isn't it?" Karrie called to them as they walked down the hall.

Rob pulled CJ up short in his surprise. He turned to stare at her.

"You...you've got a roast? How? All of the stores and all of the farms are empty, closed, or gone."

"Oh, there's still good hunting around here. As a matter of fact," Karrie jutted her chin at her son, "CJ just brought in a catch this morning. Carl's got traps all over the neighborhood."

Rob allowed CJ to pull him farther down the hall, but his face was still pinched in disbelief. Karrie could hear CJ prattling on and on about his hunting adventures, but Rob only responded with muffled grunts. She laughed and began to prepare dinner.

Three hours later, Rob sat back on the sofa and patted his full belly.

"Karrie, I haven't had that good of a meal since Annie was alive. I think I'm going to burst."

"The secret is in how you cook it. You've got to cook low and slow to get the roast fork tender."

"How much do you guys have?"

"We've got a freezer full. You're welcome to come over whenever you want. We can even give you some to take home. We also grow our own veggies in the back, and you can have some of those, too. CJ?"

The boy jumped up from the couch and grabbed Rob's hand. "C'mon, Rob. I'll show you where the freezer is."

Karrie followed CJ as he led Rob downstairs and into the

back corner of the basement. There he thunked his hand on top of the freezer.

"Here it is. I have a little trouble getting it open sometimes..."

"I'll help you, big guy."

Rob heaved the lid of the freezer up and locked it in place. He stared down at its contents as Karrie pointed out each item.

"As you can see, we've got several torsos, eight legs, ten arms, and a few odds and ends. When we section a body like a side of beef, it's much easier to stack and store."

CJ grabbed a plastic bag filled with fingers and toes and turned toward Karrie. "Mom, can I have a popsicle?"

"Sure, peanut. Take the whole bag upstairs so everyone can have some, okay?"

Karrie stared at CJ's back as he skipped upstairs. She turned to Rob. He seemed dazed.

"Rob, are you all right?"

He nodded without speaking. Karrie patted him on the shoulder.

"C'mon. Let's head back up."

Karrie jogged up the stairs. She smiled at CJ and Carl as they each popped a finger into their mouths. "Hey, save some for us!"

As Rob stepped into the living room, he pulled a .45 Kimber custom automatic from a holster at the small of his back. He raised it and pointed it at the three of them. Karrie, Carl, and CJ stopped eating the frozen "treats" and stared at the weapon Rob was pointing at them.

Carl raised his hands. "Whoa there, Rob. What's going on?"

"How could you?" Rob shouted. "How could you kill people and eat them? Survival? Because let me tell you, that is not surviving. That's murder!"

"It's not murder if they're already dead."

Rob blinked. "What?"

"We didn't kill any living people, Rob," Karrie spoke as she stood. "Those bodies in the freezer are zombies."

"You mean we ate," Rob paused to swallow, "zombie roast for dinner?"

"Uh-huh." Karrie nodded. "It's only fair, don't you think? They eat us so we should return the favor."

"But—"

"Look, Rob," Carl said. "I know it sounds odd and a little immoral. But, when the animal food source was depleted a few months ago, we thought it was the end for us. We even had a final plan, you know?"

Rob looked over at Karrie as she wrapped her arms around CJ. He looked down at the gun in his hand and, after a moment, tucked it back into his holster as if ashamed of having pointed it at them.

Carl continued. "One day I went out to check one of the traps I'd laid a while ago. Just one last hope there'd be an animal in it. What I found was, to say the least, unexpected."

"A zombie?" Rob asked.

"Yep. It was a simple snare trap. A rabbit probably could have wiggled its way out. But, you know zombies. They can't pick their noses, let alone slip a loop of rope off their feet. Well, I couldn't very well let it live, but after I killed it, I had an idea. Sure it was a little rotten, kinda gamey. And a former person. But, maybe it could sustain us a little while—maybe until I could think up something better. So, I brought it home and, after a short screaming match with Karrie," he nodded in her direction, "we ended up eating the best meal we'd had in months."

"But the infection," Rob started.

Karrie shrugged. "We worried about that, too. We're not

sure why we haven't changed. Maybe freezing the flesh and then cooking it kills whatever causes the reanimation."

Rob sank down onto the sofa, seemingly finding their story incredulous.

CJ broke free from Karrie's embrace and sat on the couch next to him. He put a hand on the man's shoulder as if to console him.

"It's okay, Rob," CJ said. "We all thought it was really gross at first, too. But, at least they're not zombies anymore. And, we get to keep living. It's a win-win for everybody."

Rob nodded but his face seemed to darken with dismay. "This hell is never going to end, is it?"

CJ tugged at his sleeve. "Would it make you feel better to play some catch in the backyard?"

Karrie stared at her son. The boy's eyes were bright with what appeared to be the pure hopefulness of youth.

Rob laughed and ruffled the kid's hair. "Is it safe?"

"Oh, yeah. You should see the wall my folks built. Nothing is gettin' in here. It's like the Great Wall of China!"

After spending the afternoon and evening together, Karrie and Carl waved to Rob as he returned home. She felt a new sense of hope lighten her heart. She prayed it would carry them all along just long enough to see an end to this undead plague.

Several months later, Rob accompanied Carl and CJ on their weekly trap check. He'd been helping them with their catches ever since he had reconnected with them. It was amazing to him how easy it was to trap the zombies. And, if by some stroke of luck, one managed to escape, they were easy enough to hunt down. Judging by their recent catches being in such advanced states of decomposition, though, the new family unit would likely need to move on soon to find better hunting grounds.

Carl pointed to the left of the trail they were walking.

"I've got a trap in there. Will you go with CJ to check it while I head up the path a little ways?"

"Sure thing," Rob replied. "C'mon, CJ. Last one there's a rotten zombie."

Rob pretended to trip so CJ could sprint ahead. He bolted forward, yelling back at Rob about being lame and old. As Rob straightened up, he watched CJ turn to face him. The boy pointed and laughed as he walked backward toward the trap.

While CJ started jumping up and down, claiming first place in the world of coolness, Rob spotted a hulking rotten zombie shuffling up behind the boy. Most of its flesh was sliding off in chunks of green slime, and he could smell its fetid stench from here.

"CJ! Get out of here!" Rob yelled out.

CJ turned and then ran into the zombie. He bounced back and fell to the ground. Screaming, CJ fumbled for his hunting knife. Rob lurched forward, pulling his own knife from an ankle sheath. He couldn't risk using his gun and accidentally shooting the boy.

He ran toward CJ, holding his knife high. He thought he heard someone crash through the bushes behind him but didn't have time to worry if it was another roaming zombie or just Carl. When Rob reached CJ, he leaped forward and plunged the knife into the zombie's shoulder. CJ used that time to scuttle away to safety. From the corner of his eye, Rob saw Carl scoop up his son just as Rob and the zombie fell together to the ground.

The zombie growled and clamped its teeth onto Rob's neck. He howled in pain but managed to push the creature off him. While it lay helpless on its back, Rob pulled out a gun from his leg holster. He raised it just as the zombie sat up. Pressing it to the creature's temple, Rob pulled the trigger.

With the zombie now dead, Rob shrugged off his jacket and pressed it against the wound at his neck. Rivulets of blood ran down the front of his blue shirt, staining it with lines of No matter how much pressure he applied against the bite, Rob couldn't stop the bleeding. He looked at Carl, and his heart filled with regret. But, he also felt his muscles relax into a calm acceptance.

"Is CJ okay?"

Carl nodded and hugged the boy close. "I'm so sorry, Rob."

"It's all right. I'm not scared. I'll finally get to be with Annie again."

Rob coughed into his hand. He pulled it away and squinted at the bright glistening blood. He wiped it on his pants and motioned to his friend.

"Carl, I need to tell you something."

He coughed again, and Carl kept his distance until he finished with his coughing fit. Once Rob had quieted down, Carl told CJ to stay put. He walked to Rob and knelt beside him.

"What is it?"

"It's a request, actually. Something I want you to do. Something I need you to do."

Later that evening, Karrie, Carl, and CJ conducted a small funeral. CJ wrote Rob's and Annie's names on a small plaque and hung it in the backyard. The three of them held a barbeque to honor their deceased friend. As Carl watched the sunset, Karrie turned to watch CJ as he ran out into the yard while carrying a plastic bag filled with ten fingers and ten toes marked "Mr. Daniels." She smiled as he approached.

"Mom, can I have a Robsicle?"

"Of course, peanut."

ARE WE THERE YET?

Calvin and Jenny trudged through the rain, following the northbound curb of the Mackinac Bridge. He'd lost control of their car, sliding through a metal guard rail and then into a pillar of the north tower of the bridge, crumpling the entire front end. Now, it wouldn't start. They had no choice but to walk the one-and-a-half miles of suspended concrete through a heavy downpour to get to the Upper Peninsula.

No one stopped to help them. Even though Calvin stuck out his thumb to catch the attention of passing vehicles, the few cars that approached seemed to pick up speed as soon as the couple came into view.

Perhaps their dark clothing made it difficult to be seen through the rain, so Calvin waved his arm up and down, but that didn't garner any better response to his plea. Jenny wrapped her arms around her chest in a futile attempt to warm herself.

"Oh, Calvin. I don't know if I can walk all the way across the bridge."

He put his arm around her as they continued to walk. "Don't worry, doll. I'm sure a chariot will come to our rescue soon. I can feel it. By the end of the night, we'll have a big laugh about this whole mess. It'll be one big tickle."

Calvin stuck his thumb out again when he heard another car approach, but it, too, zipped past them without slowing down. He couldn't understand it. He'd never encountered so many unfriendly motorists before.

He looked down at Jenny. By the time they got to the engagement party, she would be soaked through from her thin raincoat all the way down to the layers of petticoats under her pink brocade and lace dress. Her poodle-styled hairdo had already begun to frizz from the rain, and her white gloves stuck like sopping notepaper to her hands and were translucent against her skin.

Calvin's own clothes were no better. His grey flannel suit weighed heavier on him with each minute they remained outside. His black leather shoes squished with every step. At least his fedora kept the rain out of his eyes as he stared ahead, trying to see the end of the bridge through the downpour, though he knew it lay nearly two miles away. He only hoped they'd catch a ride before they each caught their deaths.

"Holy shit! Did you see that?" Steve yelled as his friend, Rob, drove them across the Mackinac Bridge.

"It was a couple, right?"

"Uh, yeah. But, did you get a good look at them? They were covered in blood like they'd stood in front of the wood chipper in that movie *Fargo*."

Rob squinted at his rearview mirror. "I wonder if they were Calvin and Jenny Whitmore."

Steve turned to look at Rob, his eyebrows knitted together in a frown. "Who?"

"Local ghost story that goes back to 1959, I think. It was

pouring rain like tonight. Crashed their car into the north tower. Died instantly."

"Are you trying to tell me those were the ghosts of Carl and Susie Whatsum?" Steve asked.

"Calvin and Jenny."

"Whatever, dude."

"I'm not trying to tell you anything," Rob said. "But, I've heard stories from people who've seen them. Sometimes, they're covered in blood, like how you saw them. But, mostly, they just look like a young couple straight out of the 1950s trying to make their way across the bridge."

Steve looked out the back window for a few moments before turning to face forward again.

"Huh. Maybe they're still trying to get to that party."

Rob nodded. "Maybe."

AND ON THE EIGHTH DAY HE...
OOPS

"I'm bored."

"Me, too. What do you want to do?"

"Universe?"

"Nah."

"Galaxy?"

"Nah."

"New solar system?"

"Hmm. How many planets?"

"How about nine?"

"You don't think that's too many?"

"We can always change our minds later."

"True. How many suns?"

"Just one. And, we can only put life on one planet this time."

"Oh, come on. Why?"

"Have you forgotten the Glavexion system meltdown?"

"Right. I'd almost forgotten. Okay, just one planet. How about the third one?"

"Why that one?"

"Why not?"

"Fair enough," the god replied.

"Can we make life forms that look like us again?" the goddess asked.

He shrugged. "Sure, why not? It's been a few millennia."

She clapped her hands. "Good! You work on the male form this time, though. I don't think I got it quite right on that last world."

"Yeah, putting the sex organs at mid-chest was not a good idea. They should be a little less conspicuous."

They shared a laugh as they collected the elements needed to create a brand-new solar system.

"And so, in God's ultimate wisdom, He created the world. And all of the people, animals, plants, and the very planet itself exist only at His discretion."

An explosion reverberated outside the school. Mr. Anders slid his gaze toward the windows and then looked back to the group of young children. He smiled to hide his fear.

A young boy raised his hand.

"Yes, Alec?"

The boy pointed out the window. "Did God do that?"

"No, that is a manmade problem. God would never hurt his creations on purpose."

Alec seemed content with the explanation and Mr. Anders continued the lesson.

"God has a purpose for everything. We may not know what it is but don't worry, children. He will provide everything when the time is right."

Another explosion rocked the windows. A high-pitched scream, followed by a chorus of cheers, floated on the afternoon breeze. The gangs were getting closer. Soon, they'd be at the school walls. God help them all if they got inside.

The children squirmed and whimpered with fear. He

needed to distract them until the roving gangs grew tired of their destructive games and moved downtown to find better entertainment.

"All right, everyone. Go to your desks and get your workbooks and crayons. Then come back to the circle, and you can draw pictures of what you think is God's greatest creation."

The Sunday school class dispersed. Each child got their supplies, then returned to the middle of the room, plopped down, and began to draw. A few students looked at the windows from time to time but most became absorbed in their individual drawings and forgot about the world outside.

"Why did you do that?"

"Doesn't he look more, I don't know, symmetrical or something?"

"I guess, but they don't actually serve a purpose, do they?"

"No," he answered.

"Then why put them on a male? Do they produce milk?"

"Fine. But the nipples stay."

She rolled her eyes at him and then turned back to the animal she was creating. She'd already finished her sentient life form and so had begun to work on plants and animals.

"What's that?" he asked.

"Do you like it?"

"Sure, but doesn't it need bigger wings if it's going to fly?"

"It doesn't fly."

"I don't get it."

She sighed. "I want something that's shaped like it could fly but can't. Maybe it'll be a good swimmer."

"All right but it's sort of drab. Don't you want to add a little color?"

"I like the simplicity of black and white."

"Whatever."

"Well, what are you working on, now that you've 'perfected' your sentient being?"

Her voice dripped with derision, and she knew it would make him angry. He smacked her on the back of the head, then turned to the creature he'd started.

"It's going to be great. See here? I've webbed its feet so it can move easily through the water. The wings will allow it to fly. The beak will help it to dig through hard surfaces to get to food or defend itself."

She studied the small animal. It was rather ingenious. She was angry about the slap, though, so she laid a hand on the creature and it dissolved into a puddle of blood, bones, and fur.

"I'm making everything that can fly. Try again."

Furious, he grabbed a handful of her hair and threw her down. She tried to kick him, but he sidestepped her effort and then launched himself on top of her. As they tussled and rolled, their creations flew left and right. Limbs broke, blood spilled, and the water sloshed around them.

By the time they'd finished fighting, not only had their life forms been destroyed but the planet itself was a ball of burning gases. As they watched, the fiery orb expanded and contracted, then finally stabilized.

She looked at him. "So, sun's finished."

"Yeah, guess so. Uh, let's get to work on the planets."

"Sounds good."

Dr. Daly looked through the telescope eyepiece. He aimed it at a quadrant of space just on the other side of Mars.

"Are you recording the data, Dr. Marrinton?"

Dr. Marrinton tapped at the computer keyboard. "Yes, it's recording now. It's—"

She left her unfinished thought hanging in the air.

"What's wrong?" Dr. Daly asked.

"Oh, my God."

Daly ran from the platform, leaped down a handful of steps, then moved to her side. He stared at the screen.

"Oh my God," he echoed.

"It's accelerating faster than we anticipated, John."

"We don't have even a few years, do we?"

"No," she answered. "A few months, maybe, but that's it."

He collapsed into the chair next to her and cradled his head in his hands.

"We have to tell the president," Sheila said.

John snapped his head up. "Are you fucking crazy, Sheila?"

"We have to tell someone. People need to know!"

"Why? So they can ramp up their looting, raping, and murdering?"

He held up his hands, shaking and pointing his fingers like a bad parody of a late-night infomercial pitchman.

"Hey, folks, remember when we said the world would end three years from now? Well, we were off by about two years and nine months. So, if you ever wanted to have sex with your neighbor, or put a big screen TV in your living room, don't wait. Act now, because we'll all be dead in ninety days!"

"John, we need—"

"Sheila, shut up! There's no reason to say anything. Everyone already knows we're going to die. As far as I'm concerned, the sooner this shitty little planet blows up, the better."

She pushed her chair back as she stood.

"Well, you can be a coward, John, but I intend to inform the president."

When she turned her back on him to make the call, John grabbed the wireless keyboard off the desk. Before she could punch in a single number on the nearby phone, he cracked the keyboard against her skull. Sheila dropped the phone, stunned, and John hit her again.

A rain of tiny black plastic squares fell to the floor as the keyboard shattered and Sheila collapsed. John threw the remains of the keyboard to the side. He spotted a heavy microscope two desks over.

He ran to it, hefted its weight, then moved back to Sheila. She had managed to crawl a couple of feet away. Before she could escape, John brought the scope down onto her skull, crushing her brain and all knowledge of their impending doom to a gelatinous mass that resembled a burst overripe tomato. He slammed the scope against her head twice more before he released it. His breath came in heavy ragged gasps as spittle slipped down his chin.

John decided he couldn't let anyone else know about the new destruction timetable, and so he set about the lab, destroying all of the equipment. Once he was finished, he would go home, eat a rare slab of sirloin steak, smoke a Cuban cigar, drink a bottle of scotch, and then blow his fucking brains out all over his living room.

"I think the population is getting out of control," the goddess said.

"I know. What should we do? Kill 'em all?"

"What? That's where you go first? Sheesh, what kind of father figure did you have?"

The god laughed. "Ha! Good one."

The goddess smiled. "I can manage a few good quips every now and again. Anyway, about the planet's population..."

"What's your idea?"

"Why not throw down a plague? It's always been reliable in

the past, though it's a bit irksome when the humans attribute our work to this other God."

The god rolled his eyes. "Why do you care? By tomorrow, you'll be working on your next project and they'll create some other entity to worship."

She shrugged. "I suppose you're right, but let's give them something nasty."

"Should we create one big plague or various forms so they don't know what's what?"

"Oh, I like where you're going with that. We can have a mild form, one severe, and a colossal, vile plague. All fatal though, right?"

"We can't kill everyone. Just need to thin the herd a bit," he said.

"Fine."

She picked up a clay model of a human and pointed to different areas of its body as she thought up symptoms for the infections.

"Headache, vomiting, high body temps, aching joints. Roughly half of the people afflicted with these symptoms will die."

"Sounds good."

"Coughing, blood in the lungs, blood seeping through the pores as the tissues break down. Almost everyone will die."

He nodded, then grabbed the doll. "How about where they *all* die?"

She paced back and forth, chewing on her fingernails.

"In addition to the other symptoms, let's screw with their blood. It clots too much, then not at all until their organs shut down, liquefy, and they die in blinding agony."

"Wow," the god said. "You've got issues."

"Me? Have you been paying any attention to them at all? They're killing each other over perceived persecutions, religious fervor, and cultural differences—if you can call their filthy little rituals and superstitions 'culture.'"

"You know, they'll probably blame that other for this plague."

"And why is that a problem?"

He sighed. "Anyway, how are we going to do this? How should we spread the disease?"

The goddess snatched the doll and threw it over her shoulder as she walked away. He stared after her, waiting for her to turn back. She never did.

"Krakken! Fine, I'll figure it out myself!" he yelled.

He picked up the doll and studied it. How was he going to pull this off? As he pondered the problem, a creature the humans had named 'rat' scuttled across his foot.

She pulled the blade across the man's face, slow and deep. He screamed past his rotted teeth, those that remained, and his breath brought tears to her eyes.

"Christ, pal. What have you been eating? Oh, right," she laughed. "Whatever I give you."

She'd kept the man shackled to the wall for weeks and fed him a strict diet of rotten garbage and sewer water. It surprised her that he was able to keep it down. She'd learned the hard way what feces did to him: immediate regurgitation. Same with force-feeding him steaming vomit.

Shelly never used to be like this. She'd always been the type to follow the rules, dress for dinner and church, and smile and nod as she accepted whatever crap her husband did/said/offered. Because that's what a good Christian wife and mother was supposed to do.

Once the planet fell into the meteor's path, securing its certain destruction, Shelly changed. She couldn't believe in a

God that would allow such a catastrophe. That crisis of faith planted a seed of doubt in her brain about her life's path. That seed germinated and grew into a giant oak tree of anger. And liberation.

Each branch of that new tree pointed to a new and exciting path, each one darker and more exciting in its possibilities. By turning away from God, she'd turned toward a life free of rules, free from consequences, and free of guilt. The world was going to end and everyone was going to die anyway. Shelly just needed to go out with a bang before the world did.

First, she got rid of the children. Shelly never wanted them but always felt the societal requirement to bear them. She ambushed them when they returned from school one afternoon. It was quick and painless, although part of her wanted it slow and tortuous. Another part still clung to a scrap of decency, she supposed. Maybe it was maternal instinct.

Didn't matter. Once the sledgehammer crushed their skulls into strawberry jam, her last vestiges of ethics, morality, and compassion dissipated. She felt more alive at the moment of their deaths than she had ever felt at their births. If she'd chosen this path sooner, she could have strangled them with their own umbilical cords.

Her husband was more of a challenge. She had to plan the details of his murder. It would be much easier but less satisfying to pummel him to death like the children. Would poison be better? Maybe just dose him up with sleeping pills. If she could knock him out, perhaps she'd be able to restrain him in some way. Then she could take her time.

Years ago, her doctor had prescribed a calming sedative because he thought she had too much stress in her life. The two young sources of her stress were gone. Now, for the third. Shelly crushed half of a bottle of the sedatives and mixed them in Ralph's food.

When he passed out into his mashed potatoes, it took her thirty minutes to drag his limp body from the table and down into the family room. His insistence on having the furniture encased in plastic came in handy for the first time in their ten-year marriage. The slick surface made it easy to maneuver him into position before she stripped off his clothes.

She strapped him to the loveseat with multiple bungee cords. His naked skin squeaked against the thick plastic as she arranged his limbs: legs splayed and arms extended and pulled back behind the sofa. She'd connected the restraints on his wrists to those on his ankles so his back was arched and thrust out his chest, stomach, and genitals.

Perfect.

Once the drugs wore off, Ralph's half-open eyes scanned his surroundings. His speech slurred past saggy lips.

"Wha...what's going on? What happened?"

"I put drugs in your food and you passed out. Then I dragged your sorry ass here, stripped you of your clothes, and tied you to the couch."

Ralph frowned as if he didn't believe her. He tried to move his arms and legs. Panic didn't seem to set in until he looked down and realized he was naked.

"Shelly, why the hell did you do this?"

"Because I could. Because I never really wanted to be a wife and mother but I succumbed to society's expectations."

She held up an eight-inch butcher knife and ran her finger along its edge. "Because I wanted to."

"Shelly, please don't. Think of the children."

She threw her head back and laughed until tears ran down her cheeks. When she was able to speak, she looked at Ralph. "I'm sorry, hon. I know you're not in on the joke. Here."

Shelly put the knife on the coffee table and then picked up a digital camera. She sat next to him and held up the camera so

Ralph could see the view screen and every picture as she scrolled through them.

"Here's Charlie, or what's left of him. And this one is Rebecca. I know it's hard to tell, but if you look at the clothing, you'll recognize Charlie's Star Trek tee shirt and Becca's charm bracelet."

Ralph's eyes filled with tears. As he wept for his murdered children, Shelly felt one last pang of horror and regret. It disappeared the moment Ralph began blubbering and trying to negotiate his way out of his predicament.

"Please, Shelly. You don't have to do this. I know the sweet gentle woman I married is in there somewhere."

She dropped the camera by her feet and picked up the knife, dragging it across the table and gouging a thin line into the wax and wood. Ralph continued to blather on about their kids, love, and family until she lifted the knife above her head and slammed it down.

Shelly embedded the blade a half-inch into the tabletop. It remained vertical when she released it. Ralph quieted as she stood over the knife, staring at it. Her labored breath echoed through the living room. She opened and closed her hands.

"I've always done what was expected of me, what a dutiful wife should do. That's what I don't have to do anymore, Ralph."

She turned to look at him, and he tried to recoil into the plastic seat. She felt a line of drool escape the corner of her mouth and let it drip onto the floor.

"No. More."

Shelly pulled the knife free and began to slash and cut her husband into ribbons of skin and flesh. She blacked out at some point because the next thing she knew, she was slopping her husband's remains into a large black garbage bag.

That was six weeks ago.

Since then, she had killed two neighbors, half of the high school marching band, a woman breastfeeding her baby in the park and the baby, and her daughter's former Girl Scout troop. Today, she was torturing a homeless man she'd picked up downtown, having tricked him into trusting her with promises of food, shelter, and sex.

She wondered how long she could make him last. How many more victims could she take before the planet died? A long-ago commercial for getting to the center of a candy sucker popped into her head. As she carved another deep line into the homeless man's flesh, she laughed.

"It'll be a hell of a lot more than three."

"I'm tired of this. Wanna play a game?"

"Like what?" she asked.

"How about catch?"

"Sure. We haven't played that in eons. What have you got?"

"Um," the god said as he rummaged through an oversized trunk. "Fireball?"

"No."

"Dwarf star?"

"Nah."

"I've got a cosmic string in here but they're a little wriggly."

"Obviously."

"Hey. There's almost a whole planet in here. How about that?"

"Perfect!"

The god picked up the rough black orb. A few cracks marred the puckered surface but, otherwise, it would work fine. He tossed it over to the goddess, and she caught it with one hand.

"Nice catch."

"I learned from the best," she said as she threw it back to him.

They continued their easy pace, never tossing it too hard or too soft, for a few years until he decided to switch things up. He gathered an energy field around the planetoid and shot it at the goddess. She reached up with both hands to grab it, and it almost slipped past her.

"Ouch! Why did you throw it so hard?"

He shrugged. "I don't know. Just 'cause."

Her forehead furrowed with anger, she whipped the planet back at him. It hit him square in the chest, knocking him down. It broke in half and a distinct red circle marked his skin. Though it didn't hurt, and the mark faded in seconds, he felt his anger seethe inside him.

He threw one-half of the planet at her, which she easily caught. But, before she could ready herself for the other half, the god put all of his power into the second half and tossed it at the goddess. She ducked seconds before it would have smashed into her face. It sailed past her and into the darkness of space.

"What is your problem? That might have actually hurt me, you know."

"Look at what you did to me!"

"Look at what? You're fine."

He looked down at his chest, which was as pristine and perfect as the day he was born. "That's not the point."

"Then what is the point? I'm dying to know."

They argued back and forth, neither one accepting the other's explanation or excuse. While she prattled on about her feelings or some such nonsense, the god stared over her shoulder.

"I think we have a problem."

"What do you mean?"

She turned around. The chunk of planet that had whizzed

past her was headed straight for the little blue and green world in the solar system they'd created. They stared in disbelief just as their mother approached.

"Children, what are you doing? You're not getting into trouble, are you?"

"No," they cried in unison.

"A likely story. What are you staring at? Oh, look at that lovely solar system. Did you two make that?"

"Yes," the god mumbled.

"How nice. That one little planet looks like it could have life. Does it?"

"Uh-huh," the goddess answered.

"What is that little black dot? Is it...moving?"

"He threw it at me but I ducked out of the way."

"She started it by throwing it at me first."

They each pleaded their case louder than the other and at the same time until their mother held up her hands.

"So, as usual, you two create something beautiful and then make a mess of it. There are probably millions of life forms down there, and now they're all going to die. Just because of your carelessness."

They begged their mother for help but she refused.

"Your father and I are tired of cleaning up after you. It's about time you learn some responsibility. Neglect equals loss. If you don't take care of something, you lose it. Simple as that. Take one last look at your creation, children, because once it's gone, it's gone for good."

They turned to watch as the planetoid hurdled through space toward their beautiful world. The god grasped the goddess's hand.

She looked at him, her face covered in tears. "I'm sorry."

"So am I."

Many years later, after the little blue and green planet was nothing but a chunk of black rock, devoid of all life, they turned away. Their mother wiped the tears from their cheeks.

"Don't cry, my dears. Come. Your father is having trouble with the magma pockets again. Why don't you help him? It'll make you feel better."

"Yes, Mother," they replied and went to find their father.

FROM THE WORLD OF DARKNESS

From Wikipedia:

Yomotsu-shikome (黄泉醜女?, lit. Ugly-Woman-of-the-Underworld), in Japanese mythology, was a hag sent by the dead Izanami to pursue her husband Izanagi, for shaming her by breaking his promise not to see her in her decayed form in the Underworld (*Yomi-no-kuni*).

I TOOK THIS MYTH AND TWISTED IT A BIT TO APPLY TO A LIVING WOMAN WHO HAS CALLED ON THE SHIKOME, OR HAG, TO PUNISH HER CHEATING HUSBAND. BUT AS ALWAYS SEEMS TO BE THE CASE WITH DEMONS AND MYTHICAL CREATURES, THEY NEVER WANT TO GO BACK WHERE THEY BELONG BUT CONTINUE TO WREAK HAVOC ON THE LIVING. THE TITLE OF MY STORY CONTAINS THE LITERAL TRANSLATION OF THE WORD FOR THE UNDERWORLD, YOMI-NO-KUNI, OR WORLD OF DARKNESS.

Bump. Scrape.

Akiko raised her head. The library had been silent until now. Most students were partying at various frats and sororities by 11:00pm on a Friday night. But Akiko had no interest in killing brain cells with cheaply brewed beer, flirting with the vacuous or egomaniacal male population, or risking bodily injury that can result with either activity.

Akiko wanted straight A's, impeccable attendance, and to become an accomplished musician. The last goal eluded her which was why she was at the library tonight. Her grasp of music theory was slippery at best and it wasn't improving as she'd hoped.

She enjoyed having most of the library to herself. Besides the desk clerk and a handful of other students, the building seemed abandoned. She'd wrapped herself in an invisible study sphere concocted of intense concentration and sheer determination but something moved in the stacks behind her, breaking her focus.

Sssshhcrape.

She peered into the dim aisles of books but couldn't discern any shapes or movement. She blew out a sigh and returned to her book, irritated at having her study groove interrupted. Now she'd have to start over at the beginning of the chapter.

THUMP! THUMP!

Akiko jumped up at what sounded like two of the largest books in existence crashing to the floor. Akiko felt the vibrations through her chair—and it had scared the shit out of her.

"Hey! What are you doing back there?" she yelled, not caring if she spoke above the required whisper. She frowned at the silence.

"Hello?"

Nothing. So much nothing that it frightened her. She lost a

bit of her anger as she imagined the demons and ghouls from her grandmother's stories. Despite her parents disapproval, as a child Akiko would sneak into her oba's room and beg her grandmother to share stories of the *akki*, *goryō*, or the *kasha*, nasty ghouls that ate the dead before they could be cremated.

Right now Akiko wished she'd never heard any of those stories. She wished she could convince her knees that there were no such things as ghosts or demons so they'd stop knocking.

"This is ridiculous," she chided herself. "Stop being so paranoid."

After taking one last look into the stacks, she sat back down to continue studying. She'd just recovered her study bubble when someone pulled her hair. She stood and whirled around.

"What the f—?"

There was no one behind her. She ran a hand through her hair. No coating of slime from the clawed fingers of a Dewey Decimal demon or ectoplasmic residue from a bibliographical beast. Perhaps it was time to go back to the dorm.

Akiko gathered her belongings, shoved them in her backpack, and power walked to the front entrance. She breathed in the cool night air upon exiting the library. She felt better away from the closeness of the cubby holes and shelves of books. She started back toward her dorm and hoped she'd find her room empty. Akiko did like her roommate, Autumn, but the girl was a bit too much into the occult.

Autumn loved to debate fate versus choice, chosen paths, or karmic design. The fact that Akiko's name meant "Autumn child" provided no end of delight for her roommate. Autumn also loved to talk demonology, parapsychology, ghosts, goblins, and everything in between. If Akiko told her about the events at the library, Autumn would never let Akiko sleep until all the details had been discussed and analyzed.

She pushed open the door to her empty room and sighed with relief. Throwing her backpack onto her bed, Akiko collapsed next to it. She decided not to tell Autumn about what happened. Too much studying could have induced some kind of stress hallucination. Best not to build it up any more than she already had.

As she laughed at her childishness she heard a soft scraping on the door. The scraping turned to scratching, then tapping. Akiko slowly approached the door and laid her ear against it. Slow and rhythmic, the tapping didn't sound urgent. The patter quickened and suddenly three sharp knocks struck the wood.

Akiko jerked back, pressing a finger to her ear. She stared at the door and waited. Another three loud knocks. Then three more.

"Who is it?" she shouted.

Three knocks answered her followed by continuous rapping. Within seconds it tuned into a violent pounding on her door, hard enough to rattle the hinges. Akiko backed away holding her hands over her ears. The hammering continued to increase in strength until it seemed the door would explode off the frame.

The pummeling abruptly ceased and the menacing quiet behind it hovered outside her room. Akiko stood still, hands still over her ears, waiting. As the seconds ticked on to minutes, she lowered her hands and inched closer toward the door. Again she laid her ear against it and listened.

The door swung open and cracked against her cheek. Autumn stumbled into Akiko.

"What the heck are you doing, Akiko?"

"Were you knocking on the door just now?"

Autumn frowned. "Why would I knock on our own door?"

Akiko shook her head. "Did you see anyone out in the hall?"

"No, why?"

"Someone was pounding on the door just before you came in. Are you sure you didn't see anybody?"

"I'm sure, Akiko. Are you all right?"

"Yeah, I think I'm just stressing over midterms."

"Then you're in luck."

Autumn held up a plastic grocery bag.

"Room service for stress relief."

Autumn pulled out a bottle of Sour Apple flavored Mad Dog and another bottle of Everclear. Akiko gasped.

"How did you get those?"

"Fake I.D., my dear roommate. Plus the clerk at the convenience store has a bit of a thing for me so all I need to do is ask."

Akiko shook her head. "You don't think I'm going to drink any of that, do you?"

Autumn locked the deadbolt on the door then plunked down on her bed. She patted the space next to her and smiled.

"If anyone needs to drink this stuff, it's you. Come on, Akiko. It's time for you to actually *enjoy* the college experience."

Four hours later Akiko hunched over a toilet in the bathroom, throwing up what felt like every cell in her body while Autumn held her hair.

"You really can't hold your liquor, can you, Akiko?" she slurred.

After another violent stomach lurch, she swung her arm around to slap Autumn but her roommate stepped back. Akiko spun and fell on her ass. Her stomach churned but did not project so Akiko settled into the corner.

"Why did you make me drink that crap?"

Autumn laughed and shook her finger.

"All I did was offer. You didn't have to take it."

"Fuck you."

Autumn's eyes widened then she laughed.

"Did you just cuss at me, miss straight lace?"

Akiko burped, a wet rattling sound then clamped a hand over her mouth. Autumn held up her hands.

"You wait here. I'll get you some water."

Autumn stumbled out of the bathroom. Akiko positioned herself over the toilet again but only dry heaved twice. When she was sure nothing more would come up, she sat back and rested her head on the seat. She didn't care that people put their bare butts on it or relieved their bowels into the bowl. The cool surface felt comforting against her hot skin. She closed her eyes and tried to take deep slow breaths.

Sssccraaape

Akiko opened her eyes and looked under the stall door.

"Autumn? Is that you?"

The bathroom was quiet. She closed her eyes and prayed her stomach would remain calm. Just as her breathing developed an even rhythm she heard the noise again.

Sssccraaape

Akiko lifted her head and called out.

"Who's there? Autumn, this isn't funny."

She bent her head down and looked into the next stall. She could see all the way to the showers at the far side of the bathroom. One of the white plastic curtains moved as if someone hid behind it then started to slowly pull it back.

Akiko rubbed her eyes, thinking she was imagining it but when she looked again, the curtain moved further. A hand emerged from the darkness of the shower stall. The fingers scrabbled forward, bringing the grey and brown mottled flesh into the light. The thin wrist followed and then the forearm, its skin withered like that of an old woman.

Just as strings of ratty hair fell forward, framing the glistening eyes, the bathroom door opened. She swiveled her head to see Autumn stumble back in.

"Akiko, I got some water for ya."

Akiko turned back to the showers. No decrepit creature lurked in the dark. The empty showers appeared normal but for one shower curtain which hung out of place, softly swishing back and forth. The fear Akiko had felt in the library returned full force. She spun around and dry heaved into the toilet.

When she finished, Autumn helped her up. She pushed the water bottle into Akiko's hand.

"This should help settle your stomach a bit and reduce your hangover tomorrow. I think."

Akiko struggled with the twist top but eventually cracked it open. She worried the water would reverse course like everything else but once in her stomach, her body demanded more. She drained the entire bottle.

"Thass my girl. C'mon, let's get you to bed."

As Autumn guided Akiko out of the bathroom, Akiko took one last look at the showers. Did she see the glint of eyes in the darkness?

Once back in her room, Akiko collapsed onto her bed. Her head swam but at least her stomach had calmed down. Autumn pushed Akiko's head down to the pillow.

"All you can do now is sleep. Luckily you emptied your stomach back there. Shouldn't have to worry about you choking on your own vomit during the night."

"Gee, what a comforting thought. Thanks."

"Hey, that's what roommates are for. I'll be right over there if you need me."

Autumn waved at her bed but before she could lie down

she heaved. Clamping a hand over her mouth she ran out of the room and down the hall. If Akiko didn't feel like hammered shit right now she'd probably find that funny. Soon the warmth and softness of her blankets lulled her into a light doze. Just before Akiko drifted off to sleep, Autumn returned and groaned as she crawled into her own bed.

When Akiko woke the next day, the room sat in a blurred haze of late morning sun. She rubbed at her eyes and the fuzziness cleared a bit. As she sat up her head exploded in waves of sharp pain from her crown to her jaw. She grasped both sides of her head and her aching muscles protested with more pain. She hurt all over.

Autumn sat up in bed and smiled at Akiko.

"Morning, sunshine. How ya feelin'?"

Akiko frowned at her and pushed her hands against her temples.

"What the hell happened last night?"

"You drank yourself into a stupor, blew chunks for half an hour then collapsed in bed. You don't remember anything?"

Akiko frowned. She remembered huddling in the bathroom next to the toilet and how her stomach seemed to find no end to its heaving. Then something with the shower. What was it? The harder Akiko tried to remember, the more her head hurt.

"Bits and pieces. What time is it?"

Autumn looked over at her clock.

"Looks like eleven."

"What? I slept through my first two classes!"

Akiko jumped out of bed. The room spun on its axis and she sat back down, gripping her tangled hair.

"Ooohhhh..."

Autumn laughed. "Looks like you'll be missing all your morning classes today, Akiko."

Akiko wanted to smack Autumn but moving hurt too much right now.

"How are you not miserable?"

"Oh, Akiko. This is not my first time around the dance floor. I suggest you drink another bottle of water, gobble a few aspirin, and take a long hot shower before you grab something greasy for lunch. Then *maybe* you can go to your afternoon classes."

"Uhn," was all she could manage. Akiko grabbed a water bottle from their mini fridge, drank it while washing down three aspirins, then grabbed her bath bucket and headed down the hall. She shuffled over to one of the shower stalls then hesitated. A vague memory poked through her hangover as she reached for the curtain. A clawed hand reaching out from the darkness flashed in her vision. Akiko yelped and stepped back. She clamped her eyes closed until she convinced herself that cheap booze had caused a hallucination last night.

Opening her eyes, Akiko entered the empty shower. Within minutes of soaking herself in the steaming water she began to feel better. As she lathered shampoo through her matted hair something seized her ankle. She froze, her hands tangled in a soapy mass on her head. She slowly looked down to see the clawed hand from last night. She screamed until her lungs felt like they would rupture. Autumn burst into the bathroom, shouting, and the thing let go and slipped away.

"Akiko, are you all right?"

Autumn pulled back the shower curtain. Akiko felt no shame at her nakedness as she clutched at Autumn.

"Did you see it? Did you?"

"What, Akiko?"

"Something grabbed my ankle!"

"Akiko, there's no one else in here except us. No one was leaving as I came in either. Are you sure—"

"Dammit, Autumn, of course I'm sure. I may be hung-over but I'm not an idiot!"

Autumn pulled herself from Akiko's grasp and stepped back, a scowl darkening her features. Akiko sighed.

"I'm sorry, Autumn. I didn't mean to yell. But I know what I felt and I know what I saw."

"Does this have anything to do with last night? I mean before you got drunk?"

Akiko bit her bottom lip to keep it from trembling as she looked at Autumn.

"Finish up and let's talk, okay?"

"You won't leave?"

Autumn shook her head then turned her back.

"I'll stand guard until you're done. Deal?"

Akiko squeezed Autumn's shoulder.

"Thanks."

Once back in their room, Akiko sat on her bed next to Autumn. She described the events of the previous evening, from feeling a presence in the library to the creature in the shower last night. She shivered as Autumn scooched closer and put an arm around her shoulders.

"No wonder you're freaking out. Why didn't you tell me last night?"

"I felt so stupid. I figured all the stress from studying and then the alcohol made me imagine it. But Autumn, what if I didn't?"

"You know we could do a little energy exercise."

"Oh, Autumn. Not that."

"Hey, it's not bullshit. If there's any harmful energy surrounding you we can find out. Come on, it's not going to hurt. Besides, there's no way you'll be able to concentrate on classes anyway."

Akiko nodded. "I suppose you're right."

"Let me take a quick shower to cleanse my mind and body then we'll get started. Just sit here and relax, as much as you can anyway."

Akiko never put much faith in Autumn's "new age" beliefs. Though she never said it out loud, Akiko thought Autumn was a bit of a nutcase. But Akiko couldn't explain what had been happening to her over the past twelve hours so perhaps, at the very least, Autumn could help calm her down and think about all of this rationally.

Twenty minutes later Autumn had the drapes drawn, towels stuffed under the door, and what looked like every available candle in the county lit and placed around the room. She had drawn a circle with salt in the middle of the floor and instructed Akiko to sit inside it with her. When she hesitated, Autumn explained.

"It's just a safety precaution, Akiko."

"Um, okay."

"Trust me."

After sitting down, Autumn closed her eyes and began mumbling. After a minute she fell quiet. Akiko looked at her roommate, not exactly sure what to expect. After another minute of silence Akiko reached out to nudge Autumn. Autumn's eyes flew open and at the same moment a loud bang sounded on their door.

Akiko jumped and started to scuttle backwards, away from the door and out of the circle. Autumn grabbed her arm.

"No, Akiko. Don't leave the circle!"

Autumn turned to look at the door. Someone, or something, rattled the doorknob then pounded again, louder than before. The towel in the crack twitched. Akiko gasped as the towel was pushed and manipulated from the other side until part of it was completely free from the bottom of the door.

Once a gap had opened, what looked like a thick coil of

black smoke swirled up from underneath the door. Akiko and Autumn grabbed onto each other as the smoke entered the room. It churned around them but never broke the salt barrier. For the first time, Akiko began to believe in Autumn's philosophies.

"Autumn, what is it?"

"I don't know."

No escape.

The smoke whispered these two words as it coalesced into a rough shape near Akiko. She stared in horror as it took a human form. The familiar mottled skin, the ragged hair, and glittering eyes of the creature from last night solidified before her. It held up a gnarled hand and pointed at Akiko.

No escape.

"What do you want from me?" Akiko screamed at it.

Mine.

Autumn began mumbling again and reached for a small black bag. The creature, which now looked like an old woman, snapped her head toward Autumn. It hissed but Autumn raised a handful of powder and blew it at the hag. The creature screeched then blew apart like a hundred fragments of torn paper caught in a windstorm.

Once it was gone, Autumn quickly stuffed the towel back under the door then returned to the circle.

"I think next time I'll need to secure the door a little better."

Akiko stared at her roommate.

"Next time?"

"I don't want to summon that thing again. I'm used to dealing with entities that aren't that powerful so I was caught off guard. I honestly thought you were imagining it."

"Thanks a lot, Autumn."

"I'm sorry. I shouldn't have assumed anything."

"Could you tell what it was?"

"Not specifically but it's pissed, whatever it is. I think we need help."

"My *oba* might know what to do."

"Your grandma knows about this stuff?"

"I always thought it was superstition and old world nonsense. But after what we just saw, I'll pretty much believe anything now."

Akiko grabbed her cell phone and dialed home. Her mother picked up on the second ring.

"Hello, Akiko. How are you?"

"Hi, mom. I'm good. Working hard."

"That's good to hear."

"Is grandma there? I need to talk to her."

"She's right here. Hold on."

As her mother and grandmother exchanged words in Japanese, Akiko gave a thumbs-up to Autumn who was creating a salt water solution for the whole door. Akiko heard some rattling on the other end of the line as her grandmother put the phone to her ear.

"Akiko? Is that you?"

"Yes, *Obaasan*. How are you?"

"Did you really call to ask me how I'm doing?"

Akiko smiled. She never could get anything past her grandma.

"No. I, uh...wow, I don't even know how to ask this."

"Just say it. The faster you do the easier it will be."

"Okay. Have you ever encountered a dark entity before? Maybe one that looks like an old woman?"

Aside from heavy anxious breathing, her grandmother said nothing.

"*Obaasan*? Are you still there?"

"Yes, Akiko. I'm here."

"You think I'm crazy don't you?"

"Where did you see this entity?"

"I only heard it the first time. Then I saw it in the bathroom last night and it just left my room a few minutes ago."

"Did it say anything?"

"It said 'no escape' and 'mine'. I don't really know what it meant."

"Akiko, listen to me very carefully. You can't stay at school. Come home where I can protect you."

"Wait, what? What are you talking about?"

"It knows where you are now. You are not safe. Come home."

"What about Autumn? It knows about her, too."

"It doesn't want that *gaijin*. It wants you."

"How do you know that?"

"You have to trust me, *mago*."

"But what about school, my midterms—"

"You can always go back but you'll need to survive first."

Akiko heard some heated Japanese shared between her mother and grandmother and then her mother was on the line.

"Akiko? Just do as your grandmother says. We'll worry about school later."

Akiko could feel a panic surge through her chest.

"Yes, *okaasan*. I'll come home as soon as I can."

There was silence on the phone again and Akiko thought her mother had already hung up.

"Mom?"

"Akiko...*Aishiteru*."

Akiko blinked. She'd only ever heard her mother say this one time in her life.

"Uh, I love you, too, mom."

Akiko snapped her phone closed. She ran to her closet and

dug out a duffel bag. As she ransacked her drawers for a few necessities, Autumn sprayed salt water around the door.

"I don't think you'll need that."

Autumn turned to look at her.

"What do you mean?"

"I mean it's not after you. Once it figures out I'm gone it'll leave you alone."

"How can you be sure?"

"My grandma seemed pretty damn sure."

"Does she know what it is?"

"I think so but she didn't say over the phone. Just told me to get home ASAP."

Once she finished packing her bag, Akiko turned to her roommate. Autumn pulled an amulet from around her neck and put it over Akiko's head.

"This has always been great for protection. I think you need it now more than I do."

Akiko fingered the delicate silver charm and smiled.

"Thanks, Autumn."

"Just be safe. Come back and show me up on midterms, okay?"

Autumn's eyes welled with unspilled tears and Akiko gave her a quick hug.

"Good bye."

Akiko thought she felt someone watching her as she got in her car but the four-hour drive home was uneventful. As soon as she pulled into the driveway, her grandmother burst out the front door and shuffled as quickly as her 87 year old legs would allow. Akiko got out of the car and her grandmother threw her arms around her. She felt the wind push out of her lungs.

"Oof. *Oba—*"

"Akiko, are you all right? You're not hurt?"

Her grandmother squeezed Akiko's shoulders, moved down her arms, and spun her around to check the rest of her body.

"*Oba*, I'm fine."

"Quickly, get inside."

Her grandmother grabbed Akiko's hand, crushing the small bones together in the process, and dragged her to the porch. Akiko winced.

"*Oba* that hurts."

"Not as much as it would if the *shikome* gets you."

"The what?"

Her grandmother continued pulling her toward the house. Once inside, Akiko's father slammed the front door and snapped every lock into place. He then ran into the kitchen, picked up a large pestle, and ground away in a frantic pace at something Akiko couldn't see. Her mother was lighting dozens of candles. Akiko turned to her grandmother.

"What's going on?"

Her grandmother led her to the couch in the living room. She motioned for Akiko to sit down next to her.

"This is all my fault, Akiko. I'm so sorry."

"*Oba*, tell me what's happening."

"Do you remember when I told you that your father and I moved to America after your grandfather died?"

"What does that have to do with anything?"

"I never told you how he died. The *truth* about how he died. I never even told your father until tonight."

Akiko's father came into the living room with a bowl of beige powder and her grandmother ordered him to spread it in front of every window and door. He gave her a curt bow then rushed off. Akiko's mother moved around the house setting lit candles in each corner dispelling every shadow. Her grandmother looked at Akiko, took a deep breath, and spoke.

"A few years after your father was born, your *ojiisan* and I drifted apart. I was more concerned with our child than him and though I hated to admit it at the time, it was my fault he turned to another woman for comfort. When I found out, I was so hurt that I wanted to make him pay for what he did."

Akiko felt her chest tighten in fear. "*Oba*, what did you do?"

"The *shikome* is an evil hag who can be summoned to exact revenge for those who have been wronged."

"Are you telling me you called up a demon to kill grandfather because he cheated on you?"

Akiko's grandmother stared down at her hands and began to sob. Akiko patted her *oba*'s back, trying to reassure her.

"Um, we all do crazy things in the heat of the moment, *Oba*. Maybe not this, necessarily, but you know..."

Akiko trailed off not really sure what she could say. Just then her mother came back into the living room.

"*Okaasan*, I've finished with all the candles. What else do we need to do?"

Akiko's grandmother looked up, tears spilling down her cheeks. She motioned to the empty cushion next to Akiko.

"Sit next to your daughter, Momoko. Though we are protecting the house, there is no telling how long it will last."

Akiko's mother sat down, pushed a stray lock of hair behind Akiko's ear then caressed her cheek.

"*Akichan*."

Akiko frowned then turned to her grandmother.

"So the *shikome* didn't return to the demon world after it killed *ojiisan* for you?"

Her grandmother shook her head. "It came to me after it finished and demanded your father, too. If I hadn't already purchased *omamori* from the local shrine, it probably would have killed him that same night. As soon as I could I packed up as many of our belongings that we could carry and we left for America."

"So now this thing is after me?"

"That is what I believe, yes. Your grandfather wasn't enough. It also wanted his offspring. And now it's trying to take you. I fear it won't stop until..."

A loud crash sounded from upstairs followed by an agonizing scream.

"Hiroyuki!"

Momoko charged toward the stairs before Akiko or her grandmother could stop her. Akiko tried to follow but her *oba* held her arm.

"No, Akiko. It's already too late."

Another scream echoed down to the living room as Akiko and her grandmother held onto each other.

"*Ie*, Hiroyuki. *Ie, ie, ie!* Hiroyuki!"

The most ghastly and sickening shriek Akiko had ever heard rang out. She never knew a human could convey such horror and agony in one scream as Momoko did when the *shikome* took her life.

"*Okaasan!*"

Akiko leaped from the couch, wrenching herself free from her grandmother. Before she could take more than two steps, however, a frightening and gruesome creature moved around the corner and into Akiko's sight.

The bulbous head of the *shikome* seemed to pulse and swell. Various warts and growths pebbled its mottled skin and its large round eyes bulged from their sockets. The long black hair, streaked with white and reaching down to the creature's feet, fluttered around its body as if playing on an invisible breeze. It held up a wrinkled hand and pointed at Akiko. Its voice cracked with ancient evil.

Watashi no mono.

One jagged nail brushed Akiko's cheek sending blistering white hot pain across her flesh. Akiko screamed as her knees buckled and she crumpled to the floor, her breathing heavy and labored. Her grandmother grabbed an *omamori* from the folds of her sweater and brandished it at the *shikome*.

The creature stared at the brightly colored amulet and laughed, a sound like gravel rolling through a hollow log. It swung its arm around and struck Akiko's grandmother across the face, knocking her down. It turned back to Akiko and grabbed her leg.

Watashi no mono.

As Akiko screamed in terror, the *shikome* dragged her prize back upstairs. *Oba* tried to crawl after them but the pain radiating through her body kept her immobilized. She wept as she listened to the thumping protests of Akiko's struggles. A door slammed upstairs and Akiko's final muffled scream chilled *Oba* as she waited for the creature to return and drag her off to death as well.

Oba sat in the front row at the wake. White flowers adorned the Buddhist temple and the three caskets containing her son, daughter in law, and granddaughter. She clutched her *juzu* as the priest chanted. She had brought the *shikome* upon them. It should have taken her instead.

Tears streaked down her face as her fingers moved across each bead. When it was time to light the incense, *Oba* shambled over to her son's casket. As she reached forward she caught movement from the corner of her eye. She turned her head to look up at the ceiling and saw the *shikome* hovering in the corner, pointing its clawed finger at her.

Owari.

Oba nodded her head, a strange sense of calm washing over her body. She dropped her prayer beads to the floor as she turned to face the creature. She hoped her end would be swift as the *shikome* rushed forward.

January 3, 1627

 Brother Luc stood over the mutilated bodies of Francois and Pierre. Their blood painted the stone floor and walls of the passageway and mingled with the sweat dripping down his naked body. He clutched a rough hatchet in his hand and heaved exhausted breaths.

"*Memento mori*. He has spoken."

Luc closed his eyes and tilted his head back, smiling.

"Praise His name—"

He never saw Brother Abelard walk up behind him with the plank of wood. He slammed it against Luc's head and the bloody man crumpled to the ground. Abelard stood over his comrade as the head of the order, Pere Ferrand, made the sign of the cross and gave last rights to Francois and Pierre.

 When Ferrand finished, he turned to Luc who had just begun to stir and moan.

 "Brother Abelard, please assist Luc to the infirmary. Make sure Brother Edmond sees to his needs. After all of this, I don't want his recovery compromised."

 "Yes, Ferrand."

Abelard left the passage and returned minutes later with Edmond and Charles. It took the three of them to lift Luc and carry him off. He groaned again, still weak and disoriented but offered no resistance.

Pere Ferrand looked back at the mutilated corpses. As much as their deaths pained him, he understood the need for their sacrifices. Since the start of their order seven years earlier, Ferrand had been imprinted with the importance of their holy purpose. The Hermits of St. Paul were put here by God as a reminder to humanity of their frailty and mortality.

He crossed himself again, mumbled a quick prayer for the dead then went in search of help to clean up the carnage.

December 26, 1626

"Report, Brother Bedell."

Pere Ferrand sat behind a large wooden table, Brothers Abelard and Edmond on either side of him. Bedell, his balding pate turned to the council as he studied his notes, cleared his throat before speaking.

"Most of the brotherhood is faring well. Though the ritual fast is causing sluggishness and fatigue, they have had no trouble continuing their daily routines."

"And the ones having trouble?" Ferrand asked.

"Gilbert has been depressed and irritable to the point of almost never leaving his cell. Marlon became hysterical on several occasions, running laps around the cloister until he collapsed in exhaustion."

"I see," Ferrand said. "That sounds rather typical. Anything else?"

Bedell chewed on his lower lip, tapping a finger on the open page of his notebook. Abelard thumped his fist on the table.

"Come now, brother. What else have you to report? Anything extreme?"

Bedell's mouth twitched upward in a half smile.

"It's Luc. I believe he has been affected the most by the fast."

"How so?"

"He seems to no longer be able to control certain impulses. He strips naked during afternoon prayers and—"

He stopped again, his face flushing red before continuing.

"And he pleasures himself in front of everyone."

Abelard and Edmond exchanged glances as Ferrand stared at Bedell. He motioned for him to continue.

"He can't understand the simplest of instructions. When asked to clean the west cellar, he sat down and began to cry and shouted how we always expect him to do things he's never been taught."

"Interesting. Go on."

"Brother Basile came to me yesterday saying he saw Luc inside the north transept, sitting on the floor, again naked, and cutting crosses into his arms."

Ferrand steepled his hands and pressed them to his lips. It seemed Luc would be the chosen one this year. He would speak with him immediately to judge for himself.

"Brother Bedell, how often are the men being fed?"

"One meal a day of water and a small bowl of boiled potatoes and onions as well as one meal of bread, water, and a cup of broth."

"Cut out the second meal for Brother Luc."

"But what shall I say—"

"I'll take care of Luc. Where is he now?"

"In the infirmary having his wounds cleaned and wrapped."

"That you, Bedell. Informative as always. Please return to your work."

Bedell nodded then gathered his notes and left the chapter house. Pere Ferrand dismissed the remaining monks.

"That concludes our business for the day, brothers. You have all done well during this time of the Great Fast and I know God is pleased by it. Please return to your duties."

Ferrand, Edmond, and Abelard remained seated until all the monks had left, the last closing the door behind him. The three remaining men looked at each other.

"So, Luc has been chosen," Abelard said.

Edmond nodded. "It appears that way."

The two monks looked at Ferrand who sat with his hands folded in his lap and his eyes closed. After a minute of silence, he opened his eyes and looked up at the ceiling.

"Our Heavenly Father, in His infinite wisdom, has chosen Luc to be the Holy vessel, the deliverer of His message."

"Praise God. Praise his name."

"I will speak with Luc to help him understand God's purpose for him. You two will spread the word among the brethren so that they, too, can understand and remember our purpose."

"Yes, Ferrand," Abelard said. He and Edmond left the chapter house and headed to the west dorter while Ferrand walked to the infirmary.

When he arrived, Ferrand found Luc convalescing at the far end of the large open aired room. The lone patient today, Luc looked like a lost and tired young boy. The purple bruising under his eyes made them appear sunken. His skin was pale and sallow, almost translucent against his knuckles. His arms were wrapped in gauze from wrists to elbows. Small dots of red created a scattered pattern across the bandages.

Ferrand stood over Luc's body as the man twitched in a fitful sleep. He mumbled and Ferrand leaned down to hear.

"Death...comes to...all..."

Ferrand stood slowly, a smile curling the corners of his mouth. God had indeed touched this one with His message. But sometimes that wasn't enough. The weakness of humanity could let God's words go unheard. It was up to those who could see the Lord's plan to help others see it, too.

Those like Pere Ferrand.

Since he was a boy, Ferrand spoke to God. He first heard God's whisper after his mother's death. At his father's funeral, God's voice spoke volumes to his young ears. After the fire at the orphanage that took all lives but his, Ferrand heard God speak loud and clear. It was Ferrand's destiny to help spread the word to humanity, to remind them of their mortality and temporary status on this world.

And now Ferrand would assist Luc in hearing God's word and solidify the purpose and credo of the brotherhood—m*emento mori*: Remember you will die.

Luc stirred and opened his eyes. He looked at Ferrand and smiled weakly. He tried to sit up but Ferrand raised his hand and shook his head.

"Don't try to move, Luc. You must rest now. You have so much work ahead of you."

December 21, 1626

The twenty members of St. Paul's monastery gathered in the charter house. Their appointed leaders, Edmond, Abelard, and Ferrand, sat before the others at the front of the room. Heads bowed, the monks concluded their silent prayers as they did before every weekly meeting. As one they all looked up at Ferrand who stood and began to pace.

"My brothers as you all know, tonight is the shortest night of the winter season. As is our custom, we celebrate the blessings of our God with food and revelry. Tomorrow we begin our annual Fast of Cleansing so that we may clear our minds of these earthly distractions and endeavor to hear the word of God."

The men smiled and responded with "Amen". Ferrand continued.

"Brother Bedell and I will oversee all our daily meal supplements, assuring we remain healthy during this time. But let us worry about that tomorrow for tonight we partake of God's great bounty."

Another chorus of 'amens' echoed around the room. The monks rose and moved out into the hall and on to their various chores. By six o'clock that evening, all members of the monastery took their fill of grilled meats, roasted vegetables, fresh baked breads, sweet preserves, even a cup or two of wine. As Ferrand quietly sipped from a small stein, he glanced over the gathered brethren.

Each man, though given permissions to splurge, delicately nibbled or sipped from the offered spread. All but one—Brother Luc. Luc had come to the monastery only three months earlier. Ferrand guessed he was hiding from something or someone out in the "real" world. He had been nervous and skittish at first but gradually warmed to the idea of solitude and service. Soon enough, however, his more secular attitude returned. Though he completed chores and fell into monk-like habits without complaint, his restless nature would rear its head from time to time.

Like tonight.

Luc had drunk four cups of wine and was gulping down a fifth. He'd gorged himself on too much strawberry jam and bread to the point where he vomited up the half-digested mush in a corner before laughing and shoveling more into his mouth. Most of the monks ignored him or just offered him soft smiles. But Ferrand watched him closely throughout the night, recognizing the potential in him.

As the hour approached midnight, each monk gradually finished his celebrating and returned to his cell. They would meditate on the bounty they'd received and prepare themselves for the coming fast. When Luc remained the only brother in the room, standing before the empty food plates and swaying on drunken legs, Ferrand approached him, laying a hand on the younger man's shoulder.

"Luc, I believe the hour of reflection has arrived. It's time to return to your cell."

Luc grinned up at Ferrand, a thin line of slobber rolling down his chin. His eyes swam in unfocused twitches.

"Pere Ferrand," he slurred. "You remind me so much of my father. No offense intended."

"Why would such a comparison offend me?"

Luc belched and swallowed a lump of regurgitation, grimacing at its acidity or perhaps a memory of his father.

"He's not a good man. He's the reason I came here. I had to escape him. He was a tyrant, an angry, hateful, hurtful human being."

Luc stared at Ferrand and his eyes widened in shame.

"I just meant your presence is very strong. Like his. I didn't mean—"

"Everyone has a different reason for being here, Luc. We all get the calling. Though the source may vary, I hope now that you are here, you're happy."

Luc chewed on his bottom lip, his brow furrowed with doubt.

"I...I don't know. I wish I could be more secure with my

choice but I begin to doubt a God that would allow such human cruelty to exist."

"Though we may not always understand God's plan, He never does anything without a purpose."

Luc swayed again then leaned on the table to steady himself. He clenched his jaw in anger.

"What could possibly be the purpose of allowing a father to beat his family into submission? To find pleasure in other's humiliation and pain?"

Ferrand steepled his hands together in thought for a moment.

"Perhaps to remind us what is good in the world. Without hate, there is no love. Without sorrow, there is no joy."

Luc stared up at Ferrand, his bloodshot eyes welling with tears.

"Perhaps to let us know that without suffering, we cannot rise above it and become closer to Him."

Luc nodded, seeming to understand.

"And it's not like my father will live forever. His ugly life will end one day and he *will* be judged."

Ferrand covered a smile with his hands as he nodded. Luc had the perfect blend of broken soul and need for justice. Though it was too early to be certain, perhaps he could be molded into the perfect messenger of God.

January 3, 1627

Luc paced between the door and west wall of his cell, mumbling to himself and pulling at his scapular. The skull image, bright against the dark fabric, bounced with each tug. When Luc pulled too hard, the seam at his right shoulder tore.

He stopped pacing and ripped at the garment, tearing it off. Once it crumpled to the floor he started pulling at his robe until that, too, lay in a pile at his feet. He shredded the gauze around his arms, leaving bloody ribbons to trail across the floor with the breeze from the open window. He'd never put his undergarments back on after he was found naked in the north transept so nothing remained to suffocate him.

Still he felt restless. He ran out of his cell and into the frigid winter air. He took no notice and ran through the yard, his bare feet crunching through the snow. As he approached the east kitchen, the setting sun glinted on the blade of an axe leaning against the wood pile. Luc hefted its weight in his right hand as he scratched at the scabs on his arm with his left. He smiled up at the darkening sky

"Thank you, Father."

Luc moved through the snow to the east chapel. It was almost time for evening prayers. When he entered, however, none of the other brothers had arrived yet. Luc felt the impatience crawl under his scabs and he scratched at them again, opening some of them to fresh weeping.

Growling in frustration, Luc stomped through the chapel. He burst through the doors into the east passage where he encountered Francois and Pierre. The two men smiled at Luc for a brief moment until they took in his naked body, small trails of blood on his forearms, and the axe in his hands. Pierre moved toward him.

"Luc, what's happened to—" Luc buried the hatchet in his chest before he couldn't finished his question. Pierre's eyes widened and his jaw bounced up and down. His hands fluttered around the eye of the axe protruding from his breastbone as he sunk to his knees. Luc gripped the handle and placed his foot against Pierre's chest. With a crack that echoed through the hall, he pulled the hatchet free.

Francois ran forward, kneeling beside Pierre and clutching the wounded man in his arms. Luc grabbed the collar of his robe and flung him away, Fancois' head smacking heavily against the wall before he landed on the floor, stunned. Without his brother's support, Pierre fell backward, his hands flailing around the gaping wound in his chest.

Luc stood over him, breathing heavily with his eyes closed. He mouthed a silent prayer. He gripped the axe handle and raised it above his head. Finally he looked down at Pierre, whose breathing had become shallow and rapid as his eyes rolled back.

Luc smiled.

"Praise His name."

Luc swung the axe down and split Pierre's skull in two. He lifted it again and separated limbs from torso, again and chopped off hands and feet. Over and over Luc lifted the axe, blood spraying over his naked skin, the floor, the walls. By the time he had finished, the pile of flesh at his feet barely resembled the general shape of a human being.

Francois groaned behind him and Luc spun around. The other monk pressed a hand to the back of his head, grimacing as he stared at the blood staining his palm. He looked up at his attacker and gasped. Luc's naked body dripped with blood and bits of flesh. His eyes flashed with insanity, the whites almost glowing in the dim light of the passageway. The gore covered hatchet swung back and forth, hypnotizing Francois with its rhythm.

Luc lunged forward, pulling the axe up and behind him. Francois held up his arms in self-defense but Luc sliced through them both with one swift stroke. His screams only fueled Luc's madness as he hacked at his brother. It wasn't until long after the life left Francois's body that Luc ended his bloody rampage.

He stood over his former brethren, panting and wheezing from his exploits. He clutched the rough hatchet in his hand.

"*Memento mor*i. He has spoken."

Luc closed his eyes, tilted his head back, and smiled.

"Praise His name—"

Abelard took advantage of Luc's euphoric state to slam a plank of wood against his head, knocking him unconscious.

"It's safe now."

Abelard turned toward the end of the hall where several monks had gathered, hiding while Luc slaughtered Pierre and Francois. Pere Ferrand took charge, delegating tasks to several brothers to clean up the massacre and secure Brother Luc.

By the end of the week, Brothers Pierre and Francois had been interred in the church, an honor reserved for only the most revered members of the order. Their sacrifices allowed for nothing less. The rest of the brotherhood had been brought back up to their normal food intake and returned to their usual routines. Ferrand ordered Luc to remain in the infirmary for a few extra days to ensure a full recovery.

Abelard caught up with Ferrand as he walked through the passage on his way to visit Luc, small stains on the stone the only reminder of the previous week's butchery. He held out a folded sheet of vellum embossed with the papal seal.

"Pere Ferrand, we've received another letter from his Holiness."

Ferrand looked down at the paper but did not take it.

"I can only assume it is yet another missive questioning the loss of several members over the past few years. Send him our usual reply."

"I don't know how much longer that will continue to be a satisfactory answer."

"We'll cross that bridge if and when we arrive at it."

Abelard nodded and walked back toward the church as Ferrand entered the infirmary. The bed where Luc should have been lay empty. Frowning, Ferrand scanned the room and saw

Luc in the far corner, leaning forward at an impossible angle. When he approached, he noticed a twisted length of material, the bed sheet, wrapped around Luc's neck. The other end had been tied to the metal bars on the window.

Luc had hanged himself standing up.

Ferrand stood before Luc and gently pulled down his eyelids but they refused to remain closed. The bloodshot bulbous eyes stared back at Ferrand as he crossed himself.

"Lord in Heaven!"

Ferrand turned to see Brother Abelard as he stared in horror at Luc's body.

"Not all can accept God's plan," Ferrand said as he looked back at Luc. "Help me, Abelard."

The two men disentangled Luc from the makeshift noose and carried him to the closest bed. They knelt down on either side and prayed over their brother.

"Abelard, prepare a place next to Pierre and Francois. Luc deserves to be buried in the church for all he has done for the order."

"Of course."

Abelard crossed himself one more time then left the infirmary. Once he was alone, Ferrand looked down at Luc's face, his half lidded eyes staring off into at world only the dead can know. He smiled.

"We all have to die sometime, my son. It's simply God's will. Thank you for your service to the brotherhood."

Ferrand stood, made the sign of the cross over Luc's corpse then went in search of Brother Edmond. They needed to organize another trip to the city to replenish their numbers.

THE HERMITS OF ST. PAUL (OR PAULISTS) WERE AN ACTUAL GROUP OF MONKS IN THE 17TH CENTURY. THEY

WERE NICKNAMED THE BROTHERS OF DEATH MOST LIKELY DUE TO THE FACT THAT RELIGIOUS ORDERS IN GENERAL WERE INVOLVED WITH DEATH AND DYING, OR CATERING TO THE NEEDS OF THOSE AFFLICTED. THEY HELD SEVERE FASTS AND BELIEVE IN RIGOROUS DISCIPLINE. ALSO THEIR SCAPULAR WAS A SKULL AND THEIR SALUTATION WAS *"MEMENTO MORI"*.

R oger heard a crash outside. Throwing the wet rag onto the bar, he stomped past the kitchen and storage room, heading for the back door. He grumbled as he twisted the knob.

"I swear if it's those damned raccoons again I'm gonna make caps out of every last one!"

He threw open the door but instead of finding a family of masked critters, Roger came upon a naked man scrounging through the garbage. Surprised, Roger didn't speak for a full minute before finally shouting,

"What the hell are you doing?"

The man jumped. After locking eyes with Roger for a brief second, the man took off into the surrounding woods leaving Roger to stand alone scratching his head in confusion. That was the first of many encounters Roger would have with Buddy over the years. He couldn't be sure that was the man's real name but he answered to it after Roger ran through a dozen others before getting any reaction.

Buddy didn't say much. Roger didn't know if the man *could* talk at all but he did understand basic English. Theirs became a relationship of slow speech and hand gestures, Buddy mostly pointing and Roger using small words and asking a lot of questions. Roger only saw him a few times a month but always gave Buddy food, drink, and some comfortable clothes. He also offered a safe place to crash though Buddy never took him up on it.

By the time two years had passed, Buddy became a legend, at least among the staff. The locals, such as they were, either dismissed him as a tall tale or as some poor homeless man who knew he could mooch a hot meal at the Howling Wolf Tavern.

One night, as Roger hunched over his accounting book, he heard a shrill scream out back. He jumped from his chair and ran outside, sure he'd find his new waitress face to face with a pack of coyotes or one of the few mountain lions that had been trolling the area. As he burst through the door, Shara was pressed up against the wall clutching her apron in one hand and pointing at the garbage dumpster with the other.

Not seeing an immediate danger, Roger crept forward and bent down, peering around the giant metal container. Scruffy blond hair and bright brown eyes stared back at him from the dark. Roger smiled and stood, motioning to Shara.

"Don't worry. It's just Buddy."

Roger held out his hand and the man slowly stood and shuffled forward, head down, eyes pleading.

"You're not in trouble, Buddy. Come on."

A soft smile spread across Buddy's face as he ran to Roger and threw his arms around him. Roger had become accustomed to Buddy's exuberant behavior over the years. He gently disengaged himself but wrapped an arm around his shoulders, turning him toward Shara.

"Buddy, this is the new girl, Shara. Shara, this is Buddy. He's...local."

To Roger's surprise, Shara relaxed, stepped forward, and smiled. She held out her hand.

"Nice to meet you, Buddy."

Buddy looked from Shara to Roger, his face a mixture of anxiety and eagerness. When Roger nodded at him, Buddy grinned and trotted over to Shara. She gave Buddy a once over with her eyes, a small smile tugging at her lips. Buddy leaned forward, gently grasped her hand in his own then pumped it up and down like a mad man. Shara's mop of messy curls bounced in syncopation. Roger laughed.

"You'll get used to that."

Shara laughed, too, as did Buddy. It was the first time Roger ever heard him do it. Short loud bursts of sound, like a parrot imitating what it'd heard over and over. What he did next shocked Roger. Buddy spoke.

"Hello."

Roger stood and stared at the two of them. Shara blushed like a school girl, the soft pink beneath her dark complexion accentuating the spray of deep freckles across her nose and cheeks. Buddy continued smiling and shaking her hand as Shara averted her eyes from his naked form. Roger jogged to the door.

"Oh, right. I keep some spare clothes for him in my office. I don't know what he keeps doing with them because he only ever shows up naked."

Over the next six months, Shara was the ideal employee—always punctual, friendly with the customers, worked extra shifts when needed—*except* when Buddy showed up. Those days Shara would be out back with him, making small talk (she doing most of the talking) or the two of them just stared at each other like a couple of teenagers. She did such great work the rest of the time that Roger cut her some slack. He just wished it wasn't during the busiest nights each month.

As Roger worked behind the bar one such night, he kept bumping into Roni, the current bartender.

"Oh, damn. Sorry again, Roni. I just can't seem to get out of the way."

She laughed. "No worries. It's kind of fun having you back here."

"I don't know about that. I just hope I'm being more of a help than hindrance, especially when it's so busy."

"You are, trust me."

"If you say so. It should be Shara back here but well, you know."

Roni barked out a laugh.

"I do. Seems like the full moon affects the young in love, too."

"What do you mean?"

She gestured to the full restaurant.

"Didn't you notice? They say the full moon brings out the crazies."

Roger looked around the bar. Every table was full; more than a dozen people stood waiting; small groups clustered around every pool table. An inebriated customer stumbled through the obstacle course of gyrating couples on the dance floor. He bumped into one woman, knocking her aside, and her boyfriend started throwing punches to defend her honor. Before Roger could move, his security guys stepped in and escorted all three patrons out through the front door.

He watched his servers scurry between tables and the kitchen, the bus boys narrowly avoiding collisions with everyone to clean up each station. Another scuffle broke out by the pool tables but Roger hardly noticed. He was studying the hallway that led to the back door and outside, to the garbage containers and Buddy. And, right now, Shara. A tingle of unease crept under his collar and he put the two unopened beer bottles on the bar.

"Excuse me a sec, Roni."

"Where are you going?"

He didn't answer but instead moved to the back of the building. Standing at the door, he placed an ear against it: muffled conversation and a lot of giggling. When he heard Shara shriek, Roger burst through the back door with his fists raised. Buddy was nuzzling Shara's neck as she playfully slapped at him. At Roger's dramatic entrance, Buddy jumped up and moved away, his eyes lowered in guilt.

Shara glared at Roger.

"What are you doing? You scared us half to death."

"When you yelled I thought you might be in trouble."

She smirked.

"After all this time you've never been worried about Buddy before. Why now?"

Roger couldn't bring himself to admit that Roni's comment about the full moon got him spooked. And after all these years, with no further explanation to Buddy's origins or current life, his brain started acknowledging the questions he'd refused to ask from Day One. Instead he puffed up his chest and pointed a finger at the girl.

"Why do you assume it's Buddy I'm suspicious of? We just had two fights break out inside. The restaurant is crawling with drunk customers. I had to be sure one of them didn't find his way back here. But if you had been inside working like you're supposed to you'd know all this."

He felt a little guilty about his rough tone but he didn't want Shara, or Buddy, to see that he really *was* suspicious of his old friend. She cast her eyes to the ground and stood.

"You're right, Boss. I'm sorry. Can I just have a minute to say goodbye? I'll be in right after that."

Roger let out a long breath and nodded.

"Sure thing."

He looked over at Buddy and waved.

"See you later, pal."

Buddy looked up and smiled. Roger shook his head as he moved back into the bar.

Shara watched Roger go inside and close the door. She quickly turned to Buddy, reaching out her hands which he took in his own.

"I have to get back. But you're coming tomorrow? It'll be the last day until next month, right?"

"Yes."

"Then let's plan for then, okay?"

Buddy smiled and threw his arms around her.

"Are you sure?"

"I've never been so sure of anything before."

Shara pulled away and looked up at him, biting her lip in hesitation.

"I love you, Buddy."

His smile revealed nearly all his teeth. He grabbed her again.

"I love you, Shara."

She quickly kissed him, his lips dry and warm.

"Tomorrow."

He nodded. "Tomorrow."

She headed toward the door and by the time she opened it, Buddy had already slipped into the woods and disappeared.

The following night continued in the same fashion as the previous two, though perhaps not quite as manic. A few tables sat empty but the booze flowed freely, inciting one minor skirmish. Before the peak dinner hour hit, Shara signaled Roger that she was taking a break out back. He smiled and nodded, hoping she and Buddy would wrap it up sooner rather than later.

After an hour had passed, the bar crammed with people and the wait staff struggling to keep up, Roger went to fetch

Shara since she couldn't seem to make it back on her own. He told Roni he'd return to help some more as soon as he dragged Shara away from the love of her life. She laughed.

"Good luck with that."

He moved through the small hallway, reminding himself that Shara wasn't like this all the time. It was just a few days each month she did her best Claude Raines impression but he had to put his foot down. She could meet Buddy on her own time.

He rehearsed the main points of his lecture in his head so the moment he stepped outside he could start explaining the new rules. What he hadn't prepared for was to find Shara kneeling on the ground, clutching her bleeding hand. Roger raced to her side.

"Oh my God, Shara. What happened? Are you all right?"

"Buddy—"

Roger frowned.

"Are you telling me Buddy did this to you?"

She bit her lower lip and nodded her head. He pulled at her arm but she resisted.

"I need to see how bad it is."

She pinched her eyes shut and held out her hand. Roger gently turned her palm toward him and he felt his eyes widen. Several puncture wounds dotted the meat just below her thumb and bright red blood oozed from them. He had trouble believing his friend could do this.

"Are you sure it was Buddy and not an animal?"

Shara stared up at him. Her eyes watered with unshed tears but where he expected fear, her expression brightened with a smile. The flush in her cheeks deepened when she laughed.

"It'll be all right now, Boss. Don't worry."

He heard a soft rustling in the woods just beyond the reach of the light above the door. He expected Buddy to come running to Shara's aid. Instead, a medium sized Golden Retriever stepped forward, its tentative steps bringing it just out of Roger's reach. He could see a smear of blood across its muzzle.

"Son of a bitch! As if we don't have enough wildlife to worry about, now we've got rabid dogs. Come on, Shara. We need to get you inside."

She clutched his arm and refused to move.

"No, it's all right. He won't hurt us."

"What the hell are you talking about? I can see the blood on its face. It's what bit you, right?"

"He won't do it again."

"How can you be sure?"

Shara looked away from Roger and smiled at the dog.

"Because he doesn't need to."

The dog wagged its tail then laid down. It and Shara stared at each other while Roger tried to puzzle out what the hell was going on. Right now, though, it was more important to get Shara to a doctor.

"I don't know what's happening but you need to have that bite looked at. You might need stitches. The closest hospital is in Petoskey so we'd better get going."

The dog barked softly and Shara nodded at it. She looked up at Roger.

"Let's go. But the clinic is fine. I don't need the hospital."

"But—"

"If you argue I won't go."

She set her jaw, jutting her chin at him, so Roger relented.

"Fine."

Roger kept his eye on the dog as he led Shara inside. He wrapped her hand in a dish towel before driving her to the 24-hour clinic down the road where he sat in the waiting room while the bored tech on duty ushered Shara into the patient area. Roger wanted to go with her but she refused. He was flipping through a second magazine when Shara emerged, her hand wrapped tightly with gauze and bandages. He overheard the doctor instruct her.

"Keep the bandage on overnight and change it in the morning. Make sure you cover it with plastic when you shower. Then just keep an eye on it and replace the bandage when needed. Don't forget the salve."

He held up a small plastic bag heavy with extra medical supplies.

"Got it, doc. And thank you."

The doctor glanced at Roger before smiling at Shara and squeezing her shoulder.

"Don't worry. You'll be fine."

She turned and nodded at Roger.

"All good, Boss. We can go."

Roger gave the doctor one last look. The man smirked at him and turned away, grabbing a clip board from the front desk. Before he could approach the man, Shara grabbed Roger's arm and pulled him toward the door.

"He said the wound wasn't that deep so I can go back to work if you need me."

"Are you kidding? You go home and rest tonight. Tomorrow is soon enough, if you're up for it."

Shara threw her arms around his waist and squeezed. Surprised, he patted her back awkwardly.

"Thanks, Boss. You're the best."

"Did they give you pain meds or something?"

They shared a laugh before heading back out into the night.

The next couple of weeks passed without incident. Shara worked like she always did—good hustle, extra shifts—anything that was needed, Roger could count on her. She never talked about the night she was bitten or even about Buddy. It was as if nothing strange had ever happened.

Three weeks after that night, however, Shara began to change. Her affectionate nature seemed to double. She hugged her coworkers more often. Some she even kissed on the cheek. Any time someone seemed down or sad, Shara was eager to do anything to make them feel better, even if it was just sit and listen.

But she became leery of strangers and large groups. Busy bustling nights at the bar made her nervous. Most of the customers hardly earned a glance from her but some, usually large burly men, made her angry. She refused to wait on them unless she had no other choice and then would scowl at them with every interaction. For the most part she did her job but hung her head low as she worked her tables. If any regulars sat in her section she would be all smiles but overall she kept quiet with the crowds.

One night, about a month after the biting incident, the crowd at the Howling Wolf started getting rowdy. Roger and Roni hustled behind the bar. Laughing, she nudged Roger in the ribs.

"Must be the full moon."

Roger looked up from the drink he was pouring then nodded.

"Yeah."

He looked around for Shara but she wasn't on the floor. He called to one of the busboys.

"Hey, Curt. Where's Shara?"

The teenager jerked his head toward the back.

"Last I saw she was getting napkins from the store room."

"Oh, okay. Can you tell her—"

A shriek and loud crash, barely audible over the raucous patrons, echoed down the hall. Roger put the glass on the bar and pushed it toward the waiting server. He called to Roni over his shoulder as he moved out from behind the bar.

"I'll be right back."

He ran into the storage room. Shara knelt on the floor, hunched over, amidst a carton of spilled napkins and a dozen plastic water glasses. Her body shook and several loops of her curly hair slipped loose from the bun at her crown and trembled over her face. Roger reached for her.

"Are you all right?"

She whipped her head up to look at him, her response muffled through a clenched jaw.

"I'm...fine."

Her eyes, a soft hazel flecked with grey, shifted between brown and grey and green. The color swirled as she gritted her teeth. She bent over again, clutching her abdomen.

"Unngh!"

She threw her hands to the floor, bracing her body against the violent tremors that shook her. Her back arched and contracted several times. As he watched, helpless, Roger saw the nails of her hands thicken and narrow as the hair on her arms appeared to lengthen.

"Shara?"

She looked up at him again. One eye had settled back to its original hue but the other glowed with an amber gold sheen. Her incisors extended past her lower lip while her remaining teeth popped loose, replaced with smaller stubbier versions. Lurching to her feet, Shara shoved Roger to the side and bolted toward the back door. Stunned, he stood still until he heard the door slam. He ran, bursting outside just in time to see Shara disappear through the trees at the edge of the forest.

"Shara!"

He could hear branches snapping and breaking but the sounds faded with the passing minute. Movement from his left made him turn. Buddy stood a few feet away and Roger rushed him.

"You know what's happening, don't you? Did you do this to her?"

He shook Buddy as if he could loosen the answers from him. Buddy gently grasped Roger's arms and freed himself. He smiled.

"She'll be okay, Roger. Don't worry."

"What is going on? What did you do?"

Buddy simply smiled and turned to walk away but Roger grabbed his arm and spun him around. Buddy leaned close and snarled.

"Please, Roger. I don't want to hurt you."

Roger released him.

"I'm sorry. I just want to know what's happening."

Buddy relaxed, his eyes softening with instant regret.

"She's changing, that's all."

A high pitched howl echoed in the night air. Buddy stared at the dark woods then turned back to Roger.

"I have to go. She needs me."

"Will she be all right?"

"We'll be together. Everything will be okay."

Buddy threw his arms around Roger and squeezed. He felt this might be the last time he would see Buddy ever again and his chest tightened with sadness. He hugged Buddy in return then watched him run off into the woods, the underbrush rustling as he moved deeper into the forest. Within moments, the night was again quiet and Roger stared at the trees, missing his friend already.

Several nights later, the bar sat empty. Roger decided to close up early, sending the happy crew home. After checking the locks, he headed to his office. A loud crash sounded from behind the restaurant and he rushed to the back door, mumbling about troublesome raccoons.

As he opened the door, ready to shout obscenities at any and all vermin feasting at the garbage buffet, he stepped out into the pool of light to see two dogs standing near the trash bin. He recognized the golden retriever as the one that bit Shara. It stood at attention, wagging its long silky tail. The other, a German shepherd, slowly approached. Its tail hung low but swayed from side to side.

Roger stood frozen, his brain slow at processing the scene before him. As the dog sat at his feet, he looked down into its eyes: one golden amber, the other hazel flecked with grey. Roger blinked then fell to his knees. The dog raised her paw and swatted him, accidentally scratching his jaw. He barely felt it.

"Shara?"

The shepherd thrust her muzzle forward and licked his cheek. Her tail circled the air in excitement as Roger began to laugh. He scratched her neck as she leaned against him. The stiff collar jingled and he spun it around to see a shiny dog tag dangling from the c-hook. Buddy trotted over, his own tag clinking softly. He smiled at them both.

"So you've got a family and a girl, eh, Buddy?"

The retriever barked once and the shepherd echoed him. Roger bobbed his head.

"Okay, as long as I don't have to worry about either of you anymore."

Both dogs barked then turned to run off into the woods. Shara came back, leaving Buddy at the edge of the forest, and gave Roger several more licks. She chuffed at him then bounded after her companion. They both disappeared into the trees.

Roger smiled as he wiped away the slobber. He looked at

his hand and a sudden panic stiffened the muscles along his spine. Blood smeared across his fingers. He quickly wiped his face again and more blood colored his palm. Tilting his head, he dried his cheek against his shoulder and wiped his hands on his jeans.

Touching his face again, he felt the warm wetness against his skin. Roger ran inside the bar and into the bathroom. Staring into the mirror he watched two small scratches at his jawline seep blood. He grabbed a paper towel, soaking it in water and soap then scrubbed the wound. Even though he realized the futility of it, he couldn't stop washing. Shara's saliva had already penetrated the wound and no amount of soap and water would change it.

Over the next few weeks, Roger almost forgot about the scratch. It had healed in three days, something unusual for him, but he was relieved it didn't get infected. One evening, after the bar was closed and he sat in his office going over the books, a peculiar smell hit him. It was a mix of rotten food, pine needles, and an orange scented cleansing agent.

He got up from his chair and moved out into the hall, his head tilted back as he took several deep inhales through his nose. The scent thickened near the back door. Once there, he bent low, sniffing around the edge until he reached the base where the pungent smell pooled. It came from outside.

Pushing the door open, the rich aromas of food and nature melded into an intoxicating blend and before he knew it, Roger stood in front of the garbage bins, pawing open the closest one. As he began to climb inside he stopped himself. What the hell was he doing? Was he going to dig through the garbage like...

Like a dog.

He closed the lid and slid down the side of the container, pulling his knees up to his chest. Just like Shara, he, too, was changing. The sounds of the night became suddenly overwhelming. He could hear everything from the mice scrambling for cover to the whoosh and flap of predators' wings. The night breeze sounded like a hurricane through the surrounding trees as they swayed back and forth.

Just as he was about to go mad from the cacophony, a new smell hit him. Blocking out everything else, even the noise, this scent, feral and musky, forced him up to his hands and knees. He scurried around the garbage bin and came face to face with Buddy. The retriever stood before him, panting and wagging his tail. He gave Roger a soft lick on his cheek. He sat back on his heels as Buddy sat back on his haunches, each mirroring the other.

"I'm becoming like you, aren't I?"

Buddy barked once then whipped his head to the side to look into the woods. Roger followed his gaze and saw several dozen sets of eyes peering out from the dark. One by one a collection of dogs—Labradors, Rottweilers, Pit bulls, Dachshunds, fuzzy mutts and more—stepped from the trees and moved closer. The smallest of the bunch, a fifteen-pound scraggly mixed breed, trotted over to Roger and sat next to him. It barked at the gathered canines and they each took a turn to lick or nuzzle Roger before slinking back into the forest.

The small dog chuffed at Buddy, barked at Roger then turned away and ran off after the others. As he stared after the little dog, Buddy stood and nudged Roger's hand. He smoothed the hair on Buddy's head and, to his surprise, found himself smiling.

"I'll see you soon, old friend."

Buddy barked once then followed the rest of the pack into the night. Roger stood and went back inside. He turned off the lights as he moved through the bar and restaurant. Though it was dark, Roger could see just fine. He was able to dodge tables and chairs, avoiding a collision with his bus station, and made it back to his office unscathed. Turning off the light he moved to the chair behind his desk and sat back, enjoying the comfort of the dark.

He leaned forward and flipped on the radio, the soft strains of a Mozart concerto from a local classical station filled the room. Once finished, a quick news report warned people of an increase in animal attacks. Not just in Northern Michigan but across the country.

"Dogs are the main culprits, though none have been found to have rabies or any other communicable diseases. Authorities advise citizens to be hyper vigilant around any pets, including their own.

"In local news, six people have gone missing from Oden in the last three months, more than double the number from this time last year..."

Roger rubbed the spot where Shara had scratched him as he flicked the radio off. He glanced at his desk calendar and noted next week's full moon. He wondered how many more people would go missing by then and in the months to follow.

How long until there were more dogs than people? He supposed he'd find out soon enough.

HIDING IN PLAIN SIGHT

Tara leaned back and inhaled deeply. Her grip tightened on the handle of the rake as the scent of meat wafted over her. Squeezing her eyes closed, Tara silently counted to ten and pulled at the rake. How could she be hungry already?

"Hey, Tara. Heads up!"

Forrester, the head grounds man (the irony of whose name was not lost on him or anyone who cared to hear about it) pulled up alongside her in the small utility vehicle. The edging equipment rattled in the back as he rolled to a stop. She smiled and took a step to her right as he hopped out of the cart. He pulled off his hat, wiped his sweaty brow, and returned the grin.

"Why are you still here? Don't you get off at eight?"

Tara looked down at her watch. It was already eight-thirty. She worked the afternoon shift, noon to eight pm, but hadn't finished all of her duties yet. Her dinner had distracted her longer than she anticipated. Sometimes it got the better of her and she lost track of too much time. It happened but she'd prefer it if she had a bit more will power.

"I just need to finish up this post hole and I'm heading out."

Forrester gently pulled the auger away from her, his cheeks coloring red.

"C'mon, Tara. You know Barnes hates to pay overtime. I'll finish up. You go on home."

Tara wiped her hands on her jeans then squeezed Forrester's shoulder.

"Thanks. I appreciate it."

"Hey, uh, you got a little something."

He pointed at her then his own chin. She wiped at her face and a smear of dried brown fluid crumbled against her fingers. She quickly covered her shock with laughter.

"Guess I got a little carried away around all this dirt, huh? Well, see you tomorrow."

He chuckled as she waved and walked back to her own maintenance vehicle. When she knew he wasn't looking, Tara licked the dried bits off her hand. She wiped her wet fingers across her chin then stuck them in her mouth again, savoring even the barest of remnants from her meal.

She could feel her head clouding over again, threatening another loss of control. Pinching her cheek between two fingernails helped pull her out of The Fog, as she called it. Good thing she had leftovers at home. Otherwise she'd have to get something on the way. Tara needed to keep her hunger under control for just a little longer. If she had to find something before she left... It was a small consolation but better to suffer a little hunger now than lose control and get fired, if not arrested. Maybe thrown in the loony bin.

Tara parked the utility cart back at the main grounds building then jogged to her car in the west lot. Fumbling with the keys, she finally got the car started. As drool pooled in her mouth at the thought of the leftovers waiting at home, Bob, the internment specialist, rapped on her window. She jumped in surprise then rolled it down.

"Hey, Bob. What's up?"

She hoped the tremor in her voice wasn't obvious. If she could guess what he wanted, her meal would be delayed even longer, increasing her chances of doing something risky.

"Well, I hate to bother you at the end of your shift but you've always been so good at helping me with the spatial stuff."

He didn't continue and Tara sighed.

"You need me to help plan out a new section, don't you?"

Bob turned red and nodded. This was not the first time he'd asked for help. You'd think an internment specialist would actually know how to specialize internments. You'd also think Bob's uncle would have made that a prerequisite before hiring his nephew.

"You know, one of these days you're gonna have to figure out how to do your job," she snapped.

He took a step back from her car as his brow furrowed with hurt. She sighed and tried to smile.

"I'm sorry, Bob. I just haven't eaten for, uh, hours and I'm cranky. Can we work on it tomorrow?"

He returned her smile. "Sure, Tara."

Tara could still see the hurt in his eyes. She'd have to do something to make it up to him but not right now. She sped out of the lot, tires squealing on the black top. Fortunately, she only lived three miles away so she was minutes from home and food.

The car tires screeched as she careened into her driveway, the engine popping and clicking as she jumped out. She aimed the remote over her shoulder, the soft double beep barely registering as she tore through the front door. The windows rattled as it slammed behind her.

Her cat, Mr. Bean, hissed at her from atop the refrigerator as she raced past him. He was in as much danger as anyone else and she didn't stop to acknowledge him. Instead she continued moving toward the cellar.

She threw open the door and barreled down the worn wooden stopes. Her mother, rest her soul, updated nearly everything in this house before she died except these rickety stairs. Her father, may he burn in Hell, built them to replace the previous rickety steps and her mother didn't have the heart to ask him to redo them.

As they squeaked under her weight, Tara mumbled a vague threat about tearing them out for a bonfire but discontinued her rant when the meat smell hit her. Her hard stop on the last board elicited one last squeak. She closed her eyes and inhaled for ten full seconds. When she released her breath, she opened her eyes and turned to the left.

Just on the other side of a support post, Tara saw the tall rusted storage locker resting against the far wall. How her uncle swiped that from the factory and got it here, seeing as he didn't own a car at the time, was beyond her. But it was perfect for her needs as it had been for her family for decades.

She rushed over to it and fumbled with the combo lock. Her trembling hands failed twice to open it, her hunger overwhelming the most basic motor skills. Frustration turned to rage and her shrill shriek echoed around the dank cellar. The third try proved successful and the lock snapped open. She ripped it free from the handle and nearly pulled the door off its hinges as she yanked it open.

The remnants of the middle-aged man she swiped from last Thursday's burial hung from thick braided ropes. Her mother thought rope decayed too easily but Tara loved how it absorbed the essence of each meal, creating an amalgam of a sweet, heady, meat buffet. She took another deep inhale, leaning close to the strips of skin and muscle hanging from the corpse.

She grabbed the man's arm and the shoulder joint popped loose like an overcooked chicken leg. Her teeth sunk into the rotting flesh and tore it off the bone. Drool slipped down her chin, mixed with the jellied blood and fluids, and stained her skin a muddy brown. The Fog that threatened her earlier at the peak of hunger abated and The Euphoria kicked in. This is what she imagined a human would feel when high on drugs. Tara believed it was the same for ghouls when they fed. A light, weightless sensation, as if floating in a deep pool of warm water.

Complete peace.

Closing her eyes, Tara ripped another chunk from the rotting limb. She chewed, slowly exhaling through her nose. Her moans of pleasure echoed through the basement. She let her hands drop, the stump of the desiccated arm bumping against the floor, and leaned her head against the storage locker. The ecstasy had built to its peak now. Her heart, such as it was, pounded against her ribs, the rhythm of rushing blood pulsing in her ears. She could feel her body sway and the paralysis began to kick in. It wasn't so much becoming physically paralyzed as being unable to care about the physical attributes of her body or maintain consciousness. Her head dragged along the metal locker as her body slumped to the floor.

Rolling onto her back, Tara stared up at the ceiling. The white drop tiles glowed with a soft haze despite the water stains and chew marks of the resident rats. She blinked back the happy tears and felt them drip into her ears as The Euphoria began to fade. That eventual sense of disappointment rolled back in, especially at the sound of creaking stairs. The light from two bare bulbs snapped on and a darkened silhouette moved closer.

Tanya, her twin sister, stood over Tara, arms folded across her chest.

"The older the meat, the shorter the rush, eh?"

Tara blinked a few times then rolled over onto her side. Pushing herself to a sitting position she stared up at her sister and nodded.

"I'm gonna have to get someone new. And soon. He didn't give me much today and I came so close to ravaging Bob as I was trying to leave work."

Tanya knelt, leaned in close to Tara, and inhaled deeply through her nose. She grimaced in disgust and waved her hand in front of her face.

"Ugh. That guy smells awful! I don't know why you held on to him as long as you did."

Tara glared at her sister.

"You know why."

"I know why *you* think you did. I just don't understand why you won't—"

"I'm not having this argument again, Tanya."

"Yeah, but—"

"Tanya, stop."

"But you won't even consider—"

Tara pinched the bridge of her nose.

"Please, Tanya."

"It's not that big a deal."

"It's *wrong*, Tanya! It's a very big deal and it's wrong."

"Why? Just because it's not normal for us?"

Tara leapt to her feet, grabbing her sister by the shoulders and yanked her up.

"It's wrong for anyone, Tanya. Doesn't matter if they're human, wraiths, werewolves, or vampires. Murder is wrong everywhere."

"What are you talking about? Vamps murder people all the time."

"But we're not vampires are we? We're ghouls. And we eat the dead."

"Exactly. So why—"

"*The already dead, Tanya.* We don't make them dead in order to eat them. Why can't you understand that?"

Tara wobbled on her feet as her vision swam. Tanya grabbed her arms to steady her.

"See how quickly he's wearing off, Tara? If he were fresher you'd feel much stronger for much longer."

"Tanya, please."

"Don't tell me you haven't thought about it, especially when you get like this."

Tara leaned against Tanya as she shuffled to the stairs. She would never admit to her sister how often she *did* think about killing someone and devouring them on the spot. Working at the cemetery seemed like the perfect set up. She could move among humans at a real job that just also happened to be a perfect food source. Like an all-night buffet.

But ever since that terrible day when she'd gone far too long without eating, her usual food didn't seem to sustain her as well as it used to. She couldn't tell Tanya, though. She couldn't lead her sister down the same dark path she herself seemed to be traveling now.

Tanya stopped at the base of the rickety stairs and leaned back, studying Tara's face. She reached up and picked at Tara's forehead. She pulled off a large ragged section of skin. Holding it up, she jiggled it in Tara's face.

"This is yet another problem you have to deal with because you won't eat fresh food."

Tara grabbed the skin and glared at her sister, ready to unleash a string of expletives that would have made their father proud. Her vision clouded again and she only sagged against the banister as she admitted defeat.

"I certainly can't regenerate my shell with the way I feel right now. Okay, Tanya. You win. But you're gonna have to get the food. I just don't have the strength right now. And at the rate my appearance is disintegrating—"

She went cross eyed at another flap of skin as it sloughed off her forehead, dangled off her brow bone then plopped to the tile floor with a wet smack.

"I'm not fit for public viewing."

The twins stared at each other for several seconds, Tanya smiling in triumph and Tara grimacing with humiliation.

"I'll be back before you know it, sis. Let's get you upstairs first."

"No, no. When you return, we'll need to come back down here anyway. Go on. I'll be fine. Just lock the basement door when you leave. We can't risk Mr. Bean getting in. Or me getting out."

Tanya nodded and kissed her sister on the cheek. She squeezed her shoulder then darted up the stairs. Tara heard the three deadbolts clank into place then a heavy scraping sound. She let herself chuckle as she realized Tanya had moved the refrigerator in front of the cellar door.

Can't be too careful.

Tara shuffled toward the far side of the cellar. Along with the metal storage locker, their uncle scavenged some curbside furniture for them. Seemed food wasn't the only thing scavenged for around here. She glanced at the remnants of the corpse on the floor, drool sliding across her lips. Tara fell upon it with a savage hunger, tearing and ripping at the last straggly strands of putrid flesh.

After swallowing her third bite, Tara's stomach heaved. She turned away from the dead man and vomited. Painful spasms jerked her body forward as the undigested remains hurled out of her mouth and onto the floor. She couldn't be sure but she thought she felt the left side of her face peel away and become buried beneath the rotten bile. Reaching up, her fingers traced the creases and divots of her true form, covered in transformative slime.

"No."

Tara lowered her hand to look at the yellow-tinged gel slathered across her fingers. Her forearm skin began to tear and soon fell away. She could feel the rest of her shell separating from her body and she tore at her clothes. She threw the sloppy clothing to one side and her soggy shell to the other until she was truly naked and left sobbing into the sodden piles around her.

Why did life have to be this way? Why couldn't their family have been normal? As much of a bastard as their father was, Tara couldn't help but agree with him on this. Of course, he married a ghoul so who was he to complain?

It just wasn't fair.

She collapsed onto her side, kicking her clothes away then pulled her knees to her chest while she continued to cry. She stared at her shell as it began to bubble and liquefy. Soon it would be nothing more than a circle of yellow goo which would eventually seep into the linoleum, leaving a faint stain as a reminder it ever existed at all.

The pity cloud over her head faded. She stared at the puddle and the neat freak inside her, as opposed to the regular freak, demanded she clean it up. Sighing, she crawled over to the storage closet and yanked it open. A ten-gallon plastic Home Depot bucket and ancient mop sat inside. She dragged them both out and over to her mess. That's what her dad always called it when her shell sloughed off. "Go clean up your mess, you hear me?"

Bastard.

Tara leaned on the mop and pulled herself up. She stared at the empty bucket then over at the concrete sink next to the washing machine. No way did she have the strength to slog water back and forth but maybe she could at least sop up some of the goo. She pulled the mop out of the bucket and let it fall into the puddle. Little bits of yellow slime splashed outward and she sighed. More than likely she was just making it worse but she pushed the mop around in lazy circles anyway.

By the time half of it had soaked into the frayed strands on the mop, Tara heard the front door. She stood still as Tanya's giggles floated down to the cellar along with a man's deep throaty laugh. She didn't know how Tanya did it but her sister was the most adept hunter Tara had ever known. If she said she was going out to get food, she *never* came home empty handed. Tara could feel herself smile as she dragged the bucket and mop back over to the closet.

The cellar was still a mess, what with the rest of the goo and vomit and corpse all laying around, waiting to be discovered. Tanya might be able to get the man down here but once he saw all this, it might be difficult to contain him. Tara had to get to the light switch before Tanya led her quarry downstairs. Stumbling to the post next to the steps, she reached out and slammed her hand against the button just as the first deadbolt snapped open.

Tara slumped to the floor, almost all her strength drained now. She crawled back into the darkness until she bumped against the sagging couch. Leaning against it she hoped that when the victim realized what he'd got himself into, he'd be too close to escape her grasp. Tanya's giggling drowned out Tara's shallow breaths.

"Come on now, DJ. My sister is upstairs. She hasn't been

feeling well and I don't want to disturb her with our...well, you know."

The man laughed then whispered after Tanya shushed him.

"You're a bad little girl, aren't you, Annie?"

"Some might call me trouble but you like that, don't you?"

More giggling and Tara rolled her eyes with what little energy she had. The wooden stairs creaked as Tanya stepped into the cellar and one final time when DJ followed. Tara could see their shadowy shapes as they moved closer to the center of the room, Tanya kissing the man while guiding him further into the gloom. As the man approached within a few feet of Tara, she heard the squeak of his shoes as they hit the puddle of goo and his legs flew out from beneath him. He landed on the tile with a solid thud.

Displaced air brushed against Tara's skin and his powerful meat scent washed over her. Tanya gasped, false concern lilting her voice as he groaned.

"Oh, DJ. Are you all right? Here, let me help you."

Tanya knelt next to Tara and grabbed her hand, guiding it to DJ's shoulder. Their eyes locked in the dark, each glowing a bright yellow. Tanya nodded and moved away to give Tara room to feed. As she reached the light switch Tanya paused, looking back at her sister. Tara bowed her head once and tightened her grip. The man winced.

"Hey, Annie. You don't need to grab me so hard."

Tanya flipped the switch and the two bulbs winked to life. He squinted at the sudden illumination then stared over at Tanya standing on the opposite side of the room. He frowned. Tara could almost hear the gears grinding in his brain as he tried to figure out what was going on. He pointed at Tanya then looked down at the hand gripping his shoulder.

Tara's pasty flesh shone in the wan light. His eyes roamed

up the arm. The long crevices, deep shadows behind taught tendons, and pockmarks of the surface looked as if a waxen figure held him, a voodoo doll before imbued with pagan magic. Sweat broke out on his forehead as his gaze fell upon Tara's face.

A hairless creature stared back at him. Yellow eyes swam within grey shadows of the deep eye sockets; sunken flesh beneath sharp high cheekbones quivered; ragged brown stumps in blackened gums clacked in a mouth overflowing with saliva. Its entire body shook with anticipation.

He opened his mouth to scream and Tara lunged, sinking her teeth deep into his neck, immediately crushing his vocal chords with one bite.

Fresh hot blood rushed down the back of her throat. Her entire body tingled with a prickly heat and she shoved her face further into DJ's neck. He twitched meekly as her hands tightened on his arms and she tore off a chunk of flesh. She leaned back, closed her eyes, and chewed slowly, relishing the feel of hot meat and blood mixing in her mouth like a stew. The last pumps of his heart sprayed thin streams of fluid and Tara felt it sprinkle across her face and chest.

The Euphoria came fast and hard. Like a jolt of electricity, the pleasure hit her and she screamed. Her back arched and her limbs shot out, stiffening like steel rods had replaced her muscles. She waited for a pain that never came. Instead every fiber in her body hummed with an intense frequency, caressing her from the inside out, until the surface of her skin felt like it was covered in a thousand butterflies, their delicate wings brushing against her with maddening ecstasy.

Her hand bumped against DJ's arm and her head snapped up. She threw herself on top of him, snarling and gnashing her teeth. She buried her face in the gaping hole of his neck, not knowing which bits she tore out but only relished in the glory of blood and flesh as it energized her body. As she began moving down to his chest, Tara heard the shuffling of feet to her right. Her spine cracked as she whipped toward the sound while trying to shield the corpse with her arms.

Tanya stood over her, arms crossed. She smiled, her eyes twinkling.

"Wow. I guess you really needed that, didn't you, sis?"

Tara blinked, a chunk of shredded muscle hanging from her lower jaw. She pulled it free then tucked it further into her mouth. Chewing the morsel into a paste, she swallowed it and smiled up at Tanya. Her voice rasped.

"I suppose I did."

"Mind if I join in? I mean, I did do all the work to get him here."

Tara pushed DJ's body forward.

"By all means."

Tanya smiled and kicked off her shoes. The rest of her clothes slipped off easily and she tossed them to the side. She frowned at her sister's smirk.

"What? I just bought those. I don't want to ruin them if I don't have to."

Tara laughed as she dug her hand into the exposed chest cavity and pulled out part of a lung. She watched as Tanya reached behind her head and began pulling at her shell. It wasn't breaking down but she knew Tanya preferred to feed in her natural state. When the skin piled up around her feet, Tanya stepped free and held out her arms.

"Tada!"

"Why do you do that every time? It's not like I've never seen it before."

As she knelt next to the body, Tanya shook her head.

"And why do you insist on waiting until your shell is

deteriorating to shed it? Isn't this better, to eat like regular ghouls?"

"If we were eating like regular ghouls, this guy wouldn't have been alive when he entered the house."

Tanya tore a chunk of muscle from the corpse's arm and muffled her response around it.

"You know what I mean."

Tara swallowed another mouthful of lung.

"Yeah, I know. Don't you find it exhausting to keep recreating your shell? I'd rather keep mine on all the time."

Tanya poked Tara's shoulder, smirking. "Are you sure it's not because you hate the way you really look? That you're ashamed?"

Tara slapped her sister across the face.

"Don't you ever say that to me again. You know damn well I'm not ashamed. I've always been proud of who we are."

Tanya rubbed her cheek.

"Then why do you try so hard to fit in? To hide who you really are?"

"Do you want to go back to the way it was? Hiding in burned out buildings, being chased down by the ignorant neighbors and their vigilante justice mobs? Don't you remember what happened in Detroit?"

Tanya plucked at a flap of skin on DJ's gaping neck.

"I do. That was the first time I ever saw you go after the living, when that man attacked mom."

Tara felt her eyes widen with surprise.

"You saw that?"

"Yep. That was the first time I thought that we didn't need to eat rotten corpses. That maybe there was a better option."

"Is that when you started hunting?"

Tanya nodded. She opened her mouth for a moment then bit her bottom lip instead.

"What aren't you telling me, Tanya?"

"I...I saw you. That day. The whole mom-dad fiasco."

Tara groaned and flopped onto her back. She could feel tears welling up in her eyes then spill down the sides of her face. Tanya continued.

"I knew you wanted to hide it from me so I never told you. But even if I hadn't seen it all, I never would have believed your story about dad taking off anyway. He liked to torment us too much to give it all up."

Tara barked out a grumbled laugh.

"God, he lorded the whole ghoul thing over mom and us all the time, didn't he?"

"Yeah. I always wondered why the hell he married her if he thought we were all so disgusting."

"Some people just need to feel superior, I guess."

Tara sat up, wiping the tears away as she looked at her sister who smiled softly.

"I'm sorry I lied to you about it. I should have known you were smarter than that. I just didn't want you to be like me. I was weak. I was angry. But worst of all, I'd gone too long without eating so dad made a convenient target. I hate to think what I would have done to you or mom if—"

"Oh, no you don't. Don't play that game. I know damn well you never would have hurt either of us. Dad was the one who did the hurting. He was the one who killed her."

Tara nodded. "I suppose you're right."

"Of course I am. I'm older. I'm always right."

"Oh my god you never let that go, do you? 68 seconds of more life doesn't make you smarter."

They stared at each other for a moment then burst out laughing. Returning to the meal, they shared the next thirty minutes laughing and eating, talking about growing up, old times, and their mother. Tanya frowned for a moment.

"Tara, do you think Dad killed her on purpose?"

Tara held a bloody morsel inches from her lips, frozen at her sister's question. A few seconds later she shook her head and stuffed the flesh in her mouth. She stared down as she answered.

"No, no. I don't think so."

Tanya stopped eating and stared at her sister, who continued to chew and refused to make eye contact.

"Tara, look at me."

Tara ripped another piece from DJ's body and crammed it in her mouth, no longer feeling the need to feed but not wanting to answer Tanya's question.

"Tara!"

Tara grimaced, pinching her eyes closed. Still chewing the mass in her mouth, she finally looked at Tanya. She didn't answer but her sister could see everything she needed to know in Tara's eyes.

"Son of a bitch. Why didn't you ever tell me?"

Tara shrugged. "What good would that have done? I couldn't stop him from killing mom but at least I got him before he got to us."

"Wait, what?"

"Yeah, I heard dad and his buddy, Stu, talking about it a few days before. You remember that idiot, Stu?"

"Mm hmm."

"Then you remember what a moron he was and how he believed everything dad ever told him. Not sure if he could prove we were ghouls or if Stu just went along with whatever dad said. I thought I had more time to get us all out but I guess not."

"That was the night you came home early, wasn't it?"

"Yep. They canceled my shift at the morgue after the assistant got caught diddling old Mrs. Murphy's corpse.

Anyway, you were home sick and sound asleep, or so I thought. I heard some banging in the basement and went to look and..."

She wouldn't relive that moment. Not because she couldn't remember every detail, every sound. She just didn't want Tanya to relive it either.

"I don't want to think about what would have happened if you didn't come home early, Tar. I'd be dead for sure."

"We don't know that."

"I think we do. If Dad and Stu had...holy shit! What the hell ever happened to Stu anyway? He took off when you started eating dad."

"No need to worry about him. I tracked him down the next day. Remember that night when you were stressing out and being a bitch until you had dinner?"

Tanya dropped the arm she'd been chewing on and stared at Tara.

"Are you telling me you made that stew out of Stu?"

Tara shrugged and grabbed another chunk of DJ. She winked at Tanya and they both began to laugh.

Tara woke the next morning feeling better than she had in months. She hated to admit it but eating fresh meat was so much better than eating the dead. Those meals were definitely working against her now. Maybe Tanya was right and they didn't have to scavenge their food. Sure, fresh was riskier but the payoff might mean being able to go longer between meals, thereby drawing less attention than necessary.

Tanya had been eating fresh for much longer. She'd have to talk to her about it. Tara rolled out of bed, slipped into her pink and green fuzzy robe, and headed downstairs. While making coffee, she opened the refrigerator and stared at the DJ leftovers. There was enough flesh to last several meals and most of it went in the freezer. But the more delicate tissues—eyes, spleen, brain—went into the fridge for more immediate consumption.

Tara skipped DJ and grabbed the bagels and butter. She wanted to see how long the fresh meat would sustain her before she needed another fix. Perhaps comparing it to a drug high was not the best way to help acclimate her to the idea of it but at least she was considering it. Tanya would be happy about that.

"What the hell are you doing eating that crap? We've got a ton of leftovers."

Tara turned to see Tanya flounce into the kitchen, her thin cotton boy shorts and tank top not leaving much to the imagination. Granted they were both without shells this morning but even ghouls had some goods to cover up.

"Geez, Tanya. Why do you always bounce around here half naked? It's not for my benefit, is it? Because I gotta say you do nothing for me."

"Hardee har har. Dispelling yet another myth about twins being exactly alike."

"Well, maybe we don't have as many differences as we did before."

Tanya stopped mid reach for a coffee mug and stared at her sister.

"What do you mean?"

After Tara put a bagel in the toaster oven, she moved over to the cabinet next to Tanya and pulled two mugs from the shelf.

"You've been eating fresh since high school, right?"

"Yeah."

"So you have a good idea on how it affects you and your regenerative abilities."

"Where are you going with this, Tar?"

"Just that maybe you're right. Maybe I don't have to keep eating the dead."

"Are you serious?"

Tara nodded. "Even though I still believe murder is wrong, I can't deny how much better I feel this morning. Better than I have in a long time. I don't want to go back to the old way. We've always been told we're supposed to eat the dead but why can't we change? Who says we're not *allowed* to change?"

"No, I meant are you serious about me being right? Because you never say that."

Tara grinned and pushed a coffee mug at her sister.

"Just drink your coffee. Then tell me everything you know."

By ten o'clock Tara was even more excited about her new meal plan. She wanted to discuss it some more but Tanya needed to go to work. As much as she hated to conform to anything, Tanya knew they needed money to live, and killing and eating people wasn't going to pay the bills.

They both went to Tara's room where she moved to her nightstand and opened the drawer. She pulled out a worn and faded picture, probably taken some time in the 1920s, of a set of female twins. They'd been using this picture to reproduce their shells for years now so they didn't really need to look at it. But it helped to regenerate quickly and accurately so at least to the public they looked as they always had. This incarnation anyway.

After they studied the picture for several minutes, Tara put it down on top of her dresser. Standing side by side in front of the long mirror in the corner, the twins slowly morphed their shells to match the women in the photo. Thick clear gel oozed from their pores, slowly encasing the waxy white flesh. It began to darken and mimic the tone of human skin; white blonde hairs sprouted along their arms; golden tresses sprung from the crowns of their heads, thickening and falling to their shoulders in soft waves.

Most detail went into their faces as they created hazel eyes, short noses, full lips, and just enough small wrinkles to age them around thirty years, nowhere near their true age but appropriate for this shell. They created general shapes for breasts, paid no real attention to genitalia, never bothered with belly buttons. Those details were only for special occasions. They'd finished in half an hour, sharing a high-five before getting dressed and moving on with their days.

At 12:30, Tara was sitting in Bob's office, the cemetery map spread out before them. The empty sections were marked with red circles and the one on the north side was being opened for new burials next month. Being sated from last night's meal, Tara had no worries about eating Bob but she did feel the urge to beat the crap out of him. She didn't think that was a ghoul thing but more of a Bob-being-annoying thing. He seemed to keep his distance from her, though, as he pointed out the north section.

"Here's where they're opening up. I just can't figure out where I should start plotting."

"Here's a good spot."

Tara reached across the folded paper to point at the border between the north and east sections. Bob flinched but tried to cover it by picking at his cuticles. She felt the strong urge to slam her elbow into his face and claw his eyes out. Standing, she clenched her fists and backed up.

"I'd start there, Bob. Good luck. I gotta get to work."

Before he could respond Tara bolted out of the office. She jumped into her utility vehicle parked in front of the door and drove as fast as she could toward the maintenance shed. Her breathing came heavy and labored. Why was she feeling so aggressive? Did it have anything to do with her meal from last night? She needed to talk to Tanya.

Once at the shed, she stepped out of the vehicle, grabbing her phone from the front seat, and walked around the back. She leaned against the squat structure and punched in Tanya's number. It rang four times before the voicemail picked up. Grunting in frustration, Tara hung up and tried again. Same results. Growling, she left a message.

"Tan, it's Tar. I need to talk to ASAP. Call me as soon as you get this. I think something's wrong."

As soon as she hung up, Forrester rounded the corner, the ten-gallon bucket clunking against the shed wall. Tara screamed. He stopped and held up his hands.

"Whoa, sorry there. I didn't mean to scare you. You okay, Tara?"

She hyperventilated for half a minute, holding her hand to her chest. As her breathing subsided so did her shock. And anger.

"No, I'm fine. You just scared the hell out of me."

"Sorry about that."

He stood there staring at her.

"Something you wanna talk about, Forrester?"

"I couldn't help but overhear the message you left Tanya."

She straightened, her muscles tensing.

"What about it?"

"It's actually quite normal."

She frowned. "What is?"

"The aggression. It's a totally normal reaction to eating fresh meat for the first time. Or for the first in a long while. It'll subside soon enough."

Tara dropped her cell phone to the pavement. The protective case cracked and popped off just as it began to ring.

She knew it was Tanya but she couldn't make herself stoop to answer it. Forrester offered her a small smile.

"I never was sure how you didn't find me out sooner. I was waiting for you to approach me but after I saw you with Bob this morning, I figured I shouldn't delay further."

A sudden lightness tingled in her chest, like her lungs filled with helium and would lift her entire body off the ground. She felt the tears well in her eyes and couldn't stop herself from throwing her body forward and wrapping her arms around him. She cried like she hadn't done since the day her mother died.

"Why didn't you ever say anything? I thought Tanya and I were the only ones around here."

His thick arms pulled her close, squeezing her in a warm embrace.

"I'm normally the wait and see type of guy. So, I waited and I saw and figured I needed to let you in on it. We all have secrets, Tara. I guess I was just too good at hiding it."

She pulled away, quickly wiping at the tears.

"Then you knew my aggression was because of feeding?"

"Oh yeah. You're normally very even keeled. You have been since I met you, unless you get too hungry. But today I could see it. That glow ghouls get after feeding on fresh meat was pretty bright around you. That and the angry-punching-face gave it away."

"That would explain all those times when Tanya...I mean, never mind."

"It's okay, Tara. Lots of us feel the old way is no longer viable."

"Did you say 'us'? How many more are out there?"

"Lots. I can help you hone your sensing abilities. You've been working so hard on fitting in that I guess you're out of practice."

"I remember my mom telling me she'd work with Tan and me when we got older but she never had the chance."

"I was real sorry to hear about that whole mess."

"How could you know? That happened before I started working here."

He tapped the side of his head.

"We all like to keep tabs on each other if we can. Takes a village, like they say. I started watching the two of you after that, trying to stay close. This job was the perfect opportunity to get to know you."

She could feel the tears flow again and her phone started beeping. She bent down to pick it up, holding up a finger to Forrester.

"Hang on a sec. It's Tanya. Hello?"

Forrester listened to the one-sided conversation, smiling at her.

"No, Tanya. It's okay. I'm better now. But we do need to talk. I'm bringing a friend over for dinner. I know we have plenty. I don't mean that kind of dinner. It's Forrester."

She looked up at him, the heat rising to her cheeks.

"Yeah, that real hunky guy. What? No, there's nothing going on between us."

Forrester laughed and rubbed a hand over his mouth.

"Tanya, hang on a sec will you?"

Tara tilted the phone away from her face and spoke to him.

"Can you come over right after work? Eight-thirty?"

"Yeah, that's great."

"Did you hear that, Tanya? No, really, I'm fine. More than fine but we'll talk about that tonight. Okay. Love you, too."

She powered off her phone and tucked it into her back pocket. She could hardly look at Forrester now but when she did, the redness in his cheeks matched the heat in her own. Laughing, Tara jerked her thumb toward the front of the shed.

"Well, I uh, gotta get to work. See you later though, right?"

"You bet, Tara."

Forrester turned and walked to the spigot at the back of the building and Tara walked toward the front. This was a sign. Turning from the old ways, creating new traditions, and finding out there was a whole community of ghouls that felt the same way was liberating. She couldn't wait to talk to Tanya about it. Perhaps they could start fresh, try out some new shells, do something different for a while. Though she really did enjoy her job here.

Maybe Tara could skip town and a new girl could come take her place. Tanya's cousin, Theresa, perhaps? Maybe she could even eat Bob on the way out.

This new world was filled with endless possibilities.

PRODIGAL SON

The young man spoke at his camera phone as he walked up the path leading to the abandoned hospital.

"Marc here, everybody. Well, folks, this may be my last trek up to MPH. For the past fifteen years, the city has planned for the hospital's demolition but lack of funds and unhonored contracts have delayed the long-waited inevitability. Now it seems the demo will finally happen this fall."

He stopped at the end of the trail. A crumbling structure, once the men's dormitory, sat before him and he turned his phone toward it. The image bounced as he approached.

"The hospital's campus included twenty buildings when it opened in 1952. This was one of the first erected so having survived this long is almost poetic."

Marc turned the device back on himself. He squinted in the mid-afternoon sun and the decrepit dorm loomed behind him in the view screen.

"It's only fitting that my last Spirit Investigation is here. I'll be back as soon as I set up my equipment."

He turned off the camera and tucked the phone in his back pocket. He'd already hauled his gear to the defunct dormitory, tucking it just inside the door. His usual compatriots, Dean and Sheldon, bowed out at the last minute, claiming scheduling conflicts. But he knew Shel was freaked out from the last investigation and Dean didn't do anything without Shel. He didn't mind. Marc started out alone; he should finish alone.

He wanted to get some stills of the building in this light, but before he could retrieve his digital camera from inside, he saw a man standing on the grass about twenty feet from the entrance. Steel grey, slicked back hair, tall, dark suit, glasses glinting in the sunlight. He was looking up at the dormitory, a small smile curling his mouth.

He didn't think the man was with the city or the demo company, but a tingle of anxiety dampened his brow. Marc approached him.

"Excuse me, can I help you?"

The man's smile widened before he turned to face him.

"I was just looking."

"Are you with the real estate developer?"

"Heavens, no. I just wanted to take another look at the old gal before she's torn down."

"You familiar with this place?"

"You could say that. I used to work here."

Marc took a deep breath, trying to cover his excitement. Talking to this guy would make a great addition to the final walk-through.

"That's cool. When did you work here?"

He turned to look at Marc, that smile never faltering.

"Long before you were born I'm sure, young man. You wouldn't be interested."

"Are you kidding me? I mean, I'd like to know what it was like back in the seventies."

The man looked sideways at him.

"Uh, eighties?"

The man stared back up at the abandoned building and his smile faltered. He took off his glasses and pulled out a crisp white handkerchief to clean them.

"You should have seen this place during its heyday. Twenty buildings in the entire complex, revolutionary therapy with music, specialized sessions. Did you know this place allowed more personal freedoms to patients than any other hospital in the whole state?"

"But isn't that why it also had the most escapees than any other?"

The man looked at Marc, his eyes hooded, his mouth a tight line.

"And what would you have preferred? The giant wall they kept proposing? Treat the patients like criminals?"

"Well, no but— "

"The ones that did wander off grounds were harmless anyway. Except just one–Mr. Brunner. That poor woman. Body parts everywhere before the police got him."

"Wait, what?"

The man turned away and stared off to the left. He pointed.

"That's where the first building went up. It was an exciting time. When patients began registering, it was like the fulfillment of a dream."

1950s

The construction on all twenty buildings had finally finished. Over 600 patients were admitted and checked into the various dormitories. Even the elderly, who had been cast off by their relatives as too burdensome, had their own dorm where their needs could be met. Dr. Stephen Black stood outside the administration center, surveying the grounds, and smiled.

"It's everything I've worked for come to life. I can hardly believe it's here."

The head nurse stood next to the superintendent and smiled with him.

"We're going to do great things here, sir."

"Thank you, Miss Braston. Now, let's get to work. If we want to be ready for the inaugural Patients' Fair, we'd better get a move on."

By the end of the week, hospital staff and volunteer organizations had everything arranged. Dozens of game booths had been set up near the administration building while food carts and stands sat under the pavilion near the center of the grounds. Most of the patients were eager for the fair to begin. Some became too agitated by all the commotion and had to be kept in isolation. Dr. Black directed two orderlies, Phil and Brent, to secure those patients before the crowds arrived.

Phil headed over to the men's dormitory while Brent handled the women. He moved through the first two floors and those patients staying behind were either sleeping or strapped to their beds. A few struggled against the restraints but he checked them off his list. By the time he reached the fourth floor, he could hear visitors arriving outside. With one room remaining, Brent could finish in time to enjoy the fair.

The last room on the right belonged to a twenty-year-old woman, Regina, who his father would have called "a little slow in the head." Embarrassed, her family dumped her here. He looked through the window in the door. She'd already been strapped in, but she thrashed wildly trying to break free. Brent checked her off the list then went in.

She stopped moving when the door opened. When her eyes fell on him, her face screwed up into a grimace and she screamed. Brent only smiled.

"Now, now, Regina. You know everyone is outside. No one

is going to hear you, so you might as well cooperate and be quiet, okay?"

She stopped yelling but continued to struggle against her straps. He placed his clipboard on the small desk in the corner then turned to her. He pulled at his belt, unbuckling it then unsnapping the closure on his slacks. She stared at him as he pulled down his zipper.

"Don't worry, honey. You got me all worked up wriggling around like that, showing off those pretty legs of yours. It won't take me long."

Regina whimpered as he approached the bed. She may have been simple but she wasn't stupid. And her memory was unfailing. He ran his hand along the inside of her thigh and under her gown. He ripped off her underwear and she shrieked. He threw himself on top of her, pressing his hand over her mouth. Her muffled cries vibrated against his palm.

"Yeah, that's how I like it, baby. Fight. Fight hard."

Outside in the courtyard, Phil directed the male patients toward the games. Most filed along, smiling and excited. The unenthused few dragged their feet. He approached one in the middle of the line and put his arm around the man's shoulders. He squeezed and the man flinched. Phil mumbled against his ear.

"You better put a smile on that wrinkled old face of yours, Pat, and show these people how damned happy you are."

The man whimpered but eventually curled his lips upward.

"That's better. Now keep moving."

He followed the procession and kept a watchful eye on the men as they approached each booth and participated in the simple games provided. One patient stood off to the side crying, chewing on his thumb like a kid lost in a department store. Some patrons started to stare at him. Phil sighed and walked over, putting his strong-armed embrace around the man and he whispered.

"Get your shit together, Connor. If these people think you're unhappy, that won't be good for the hospital. You want the hospital to stay in business, right?"

Connor grimaced as Phil crushed the patient's arm in his grip. Before Connor could cry out, Phil pulled him as close as possible.

"Keep your trap shut, you germ. If I have to explain your whimpering, I'll get very mad. You don't want me to get mad, do you, Connor?"

The patient shook his head violently and lowered his thumb. A local journalist walked over and asked to get a picture. Phil smiled, keeping his arm around Connor's shoulders.

"Well, of course you can. Let's get over to one of the booths and get a few more patients in the shot. Would that be all right?"

"That's a wonderful idea," the man said.

Phil corralled half a dozen other patients. When they'd all gathered, he lowered his hand and dug a thumb into Connor's kidney. Smiling, Phil turned to look at the patients before staring down at Connor.

"Everyone say cheese!"

A half-hearted chorus of "cheese" echoed into the afternoon air as the newspaper photographer took his snapshot. Phil smiled.

"Great job, fellas. Now go enjoy the fair."

They wandered back to the games. Phil gave Connor a wink before the man shuffled off into the crowd and he hid a smile behind his hand. He turned back to look at the line of game booths along the wall and saw two patients headed for the road. No one else had noticed yet. Phil looked down at his watch.

"Time for a smoke break."

When he looked back up, both patients had disappeared. He grinned then headed toward the dorms to bum a cigarette off another orderly.

1960s

Dr. Black yelled through the phone.

"I know you're short staffed, Gerald, but with the riots I'm stuck at home until the police give the all clear. Who knows how long that will take?"

"But the five of us can't—"

"You have some volunteers, yes?"

"About a dozen, I think."

"Then what are you worried about? I'm sure those of us trapped by the melee going on outside will be back in a day or two. You'll be fine. Call me only for emergencies."

The click echoed through the receiver and into the office where the other orderly and three nurses sat, hoping for some relief. Gerald hung up the phone and they stared at each other, their faces sagging in defeat.

"We're on our own, folks."

"How the hell are the five of us supposed to care for over 2000 patients?"

Gerald scratched his head. "The volunteers can—"

"You must be joking," Amanda said. "Those potato heads can't do anything."

A cough near the door caught their attention and they turned to see Craig, the head of the volunteers. His face burned bright red.

"Um, just wanted to check to see if there's anything we can do."

Amanda huffed and strode out of the main office, shoving Craig to the side. Gerald offered a smile of apology.

"Don't mind her, Craig. She's just frustrated and overworked. We all are."

"I know," he said. "We could handle the public tours coming through today if you think that might help."

One of the other nurses, Angela, stood and smiled. "That's a great idea, Craig. It will take a huge chunk of stress off us right now."

He blushed and stared at his feet.

"No worries, Angela. I'll organize the group and divvy up the tours between us."

He waved and walked off down the hall. Gerald nudged Angela in the ribs, sneering.

"Wow. Is he sweet on you or what?"

"Drop dead, Gerald. Come on, Stacy. We've got to start rounds."

The other nurse nodded, offered Gerald a sly smile, then followed Angela. Amanda ran down the hall toward them.

"We're out of Thorazine."

"What?"

"Clean the wax out of your ears, Stacy. We're out of Thorazine. Friggin budget cuts have finally hit an all new low."

"So order more."

"You're not hearing me, Angela. There's hardly enough money for our salaries, let alone sedatives. We're screwed."

Gerald and the other orderly, Paul, joined them in the hall. They both held billy clubs.

"This is all the Thorazine we'll need. Paul, you go with Amanda. I'll tag along with Angela and Stacy today."

"No way."

"Relax, Angela. We can trade off tomorrow so you don't fall in love with me too quick."

As the three of them moved away, Gerald slammed the club against each door and hollered.

"You all keep quiet now, you hear? Don't make me use this on you, too."

Craig stood in the lobby with the eight other volunteers. He could hear Gerald yelling but not the words, though he knew how sadistic the man was. He smiled at the group.

"We've got three tours coming today. Luckily, we were able to cancel the others scheduled for later in the week. It'll be tough with only five employees keeping everything in check, but I think we can help them do it."

They looked at each other, eyes shining with worry, faces crinkled in fear or disgust, Craig couldn't tell. He knew the seedy goings on when the lights went out, so did they, but better to play volunteer than get shut up in the quiet room again. He looked over the shoulders of those gathered to see a giant passenger bus pull through the circular drive and park in front of the main doors. Craig smiled at the other patients.

"All right, people. Show time."

As the tours began, Paul and Amanda stood in the break room sipping coffee and smoking. They'd checked the east wing of the men's dorm while the others checked the west. As she blew smoke at Paul's face, she jutted her chin at the clipboard in his hand.

"What's next?"

"The kids' ward."

"Ugh. Fucking kids, I can't stand them."

"I'm sure they just love you, though."

She snorted.

"Yeah, they love it when I leave them alone."

"Let's just hurry. We've got to wrap this up before we start logging the criminals."

"We're not doing that shit alone, are we? The other three better help."

"They'll have to. We're out of Thorazine, remember?"

She dropped her cigarette onto the floor and ground it under her foot. Draining the cold coffee, she grimaced then left the dirty cup in the sink.

"Come on. Let's get it over with."

She and Paul headed out as Craig led a group of visitors through the courtyard. She nudged Paul.

"I can't believe that retard is pulling it off. Maybe I'll have to pay him a special thank you visit later."

"You'd better make yourself look like Angela if you want to get any action from him."

They shared a laugh and walked over to the new Children's Ward on the west side of campus. Screams floated on the afternoon breeze as they approached the building. Amanda grunted in frustration.

"Fucking kids. How can so few make so much damn noise? If those visitors hear them..."

"Let's get in there and shut them up."

He hefted the billy club and smacked it against his palm as she opened the side entrance. The shrieks intensified for a few minutes but by the time the tour group circled toward the dorm, the children had quieted and only Craig's voice echoed through the complex.

"Over here is our new Children's Ward. MPH has revolutionized the treatment of adolescents with our new Child Care Workers, who actually live with the children during their stay."

His voice faded as he led the tour over toward the pavilion. Amanda and Paul watched him through a window on the second level, the room's twelve-year-old patient lying unconscious on the floor behind them. A purple bruise darkened the middle of his forehead.

When Craig and the group disappeared, Amanda stepped away from the window. She stared down at the child on the floor, nudging him with her foot.

"You awake?"

With no response, she kicked him.

"Hey!"

He remained still and Paul pulled her sleeve.

"He's good. Let's confine the rest then head back over to the main building. See how the others are coming along."

Walking back down the hall, Paul slammed the club against each door. A few whimpers answered him but otherwise the quiet prevailed. Until one patient, a nine-year old girl, ran toward them, screeching and tearing at her hospital pajamas. Amanda grabbed her, trying to capture her flailing arms but the girl's schizophrenia rendered her stronger than she looked. As she ripped at Amanda's hair, Paul swung the club against the girl's knees and she crumbled. Her screaming continued but the swelling joints would keep her immobile long enough.

Amanda smoothed her hair and straightened her skewed cap. She walked away, motioning for Paul to follow, leaving the mewling girl to writhe in agony as they locked the rest of the patients in their rooms for the night.

The five employees gathered in the front office late that afternoon. Craig and the other volunteers were escorting the final visitors outside to the waiting bus. They watched them push through the doors, some turning back and thanking Craig and the volunteers. Gerald snorted.

"I can't believe they pulled it off. Damn."

As they all laughed, a stooped older woman shuffled past the office. Angela pointed at her.

"Who's that?"

Amanda darted out and stopped the woman.

"Where do you think you're going, dear?"

The woman pulled on a pair of clean white gloves and pointed at the leaving visitors.

"I had to go to the bathroom, but I got lost. I missed half of the tour," she whined.

"You expect me to believe you're with the tour group?"

"I am. You don't think I'm a patient, do you?"

Amanda waved to Angela who joined them in the hall.

"Angela, this woman...what's your name, hon?"

"Mrs. Robert Leon."

"Right. Mrs. Leon here says she's 'a visitor,'" Amanda said, using air quotes to Angela's amusement.

"Of course, she is. Why don't I take her?"

"Be my guest."

"Come on, Mrs. Leon. I'll get you back to your group."

"Thank you, dear."

The two women walked toward the lobby, but Angela turned down the first hallway to their left. The older woman tried to pull away.

"Where are you taking me? The group is over there. The bus is leaving!"

"Shhh, now you just come with me, Mrs. Leon. Let's go."

"But I'm not a patient."

She struggled, her voice becoming shrill. Angela turned her head and shouted.

"Gerald? Give me a hand, would you?"

The nurse and orderly escorted Mrs. Leon to the quiet room despite her vehement protests. Gerald gripped the woman's arm and she squeaked.

"Listen, gramma. I don't know where you got your get up

here, but I can assure you it won't happen again. Not after a few days in the hole. Now move."

As they dragged Mrs. Leon down the hall, Craig waved to the visitors on the bus as it pulled out of the main lot and drove away. He turned to see Phil Rebbe, a middle-aged patient, walk out of the men's dormitory and toward the road. His hospital gown flapped in the afternoon breeze and Craig chewed his fingernails with worry.

"I wonder if I should go get him?"

Phil stopped on the rough shoulder, behind the white guide line. He stood there for several minutes, swaying on wiry legs and bare feet, until a gravel hauler rumbled over the hill. Just as the truck approached, Phil stepped into the road. The driver never had a chance to even consider stopping before he plowed into Phil and smeared him across the blacktop.

Craig's mouth hung open in shock and tears filled his eyes. Not out of sadness but envy. At least Phil was free. He watched as Gerald and Paul burst through the front door. Craig watched them for a moment then walked back to his room, wiping the wetness from his cheeks.

1970s

Sheila Roberts clapped her hands to quiet the noise sweeping the room.

"Ladies, may I have your attention please? We have a lot to cover before the patients get here so let's get to it shall we?"

The members of the Ladies Auxiliary stopped gossiping and gave their full attention to their president.

"We have our monthly 'Unadopted Ward' party next week."

A collective groan echoed through the room and Sheila held up her hand.

"I know. Those pathetic souls without friends or family are a nuisance with all their slobbering gratitude for our benevolence. But we need to maintain the charade or else the hospital can't allow us to raise funds through our weekly store front."

A chorus of chuckles spread through the room and Sheila smiled.

"And we all know how much Dr. Black loves our 'goods', don't we?"

A woman at the back of the room raised her hand and Sheila pointed to her.

"The Chair recognizes Kat Shales."

"Thank you. I just wanted to let everyone know that my crop has doubled these past few months thanks to Liz's organic plant food."

Oohs and *aahs* circulated as those sitting next to Liz patted her shoulder or offered smiles. The rest clapped and cheered both members.

"That's aces, Kat. Any chance of leftovers for our annual Christmas party?"

"I'm sure I can arrange that, Sheila. I found a new brownie recipe yesterday and would love to test it out on the group, if that suits the membership."

Another round of clapping and excited chatter filled the room and the president let the women enjoy the moment. Eventually they settled and continued with their meeting.

Dr. Black stood outside the common room, his ear close to the partially opened door. A warm smile curled his lips as he listened. He did, indeed, enjoy their goods, and not just the ones grown in Mrs. Shales' basement. As he eavesdropped, a thin shaky man wearing only hospital pants approached him and tugged at his suit coat. The doctor stared down at the pathetic patient, Carl if he remembered correctly, and frowned.

Gregory, one of the orderlies on duty, rushed over and pulled the patient away.

"Now, Carl, don't go bothering the superintendent. He has much more important things to do than be picked at by you."

Gregory looked up at Dr. Black.

"I'm sorry, sir. Carl's a wily one if you're not watching him every second."

"Why is he wandering the halls? Why hasn't he been medicated?"

"We only had enough funds for a week's worth of meds this month. It was either let those dwindle or cut out toilet paper."

"Yes, I see the dilemma," Dr. Black said as he stared down at the half-dressed patient. "Can't have them running around covered in shit, now can we?"

Gregory smirked. "No, sir."

"Well, take Carl back to his room. At least strap him down so he can't wander. Lord knows the neighborhood already hates us, and the police want us to wall everyone in like common criminals."

"Of course. Sorry he bothered you."

Dr. Black pulled a pen from his jacket pocket and pressed it against Carl's shoulder, pushing the little man away.

"It's all right, Gregory. Just try to keep on top of this sort of thing."

"Will do. Oh, that reminds me. Chief Franks called with news about the patient that wandered off a few months ago."

"Why wasn't I informed sooner?"

"Nurse Poste just took the call, maybe half an hour ago?"

Dr. Black scowled at the orderly.

"Again I ask, why wasn't I informed sooner?"

"I...uh, well, I don't know."

Dr. Black sneered and elbowed Gregory to the side. He strode down the hall toward the nurses' station. As he passed one of the bathrooms, he could hear deep grunts and curses as well as the steady splash of flowing water, the metallic clank of wrench against pipe.

"Sounds like the patients will be shorted meds next month, too."

He rounded the corner and stopped in front of the nurses' station, his breathing rough and fast. Nurse Poste spoke softly into the phone as she stared up at him.

"I'll have to call you back."

She stood, straightening her uniform.

"Yes, Dr. Black, what can I do for you?"

"Did I hear correctly that you received news on Janice Belturn, the patient who wandered off the grounds two months ago?"

"Ummm, yes I..."

She scrabbled through a stack of small sheets of paper, hand-written notes, as her face glowed bright crimson.

"I had the message right here a minute ago."

She plucked one note from the pile and held it aloft.

"Ah! Here it is. I was just going—"

Dr. Black snatched it from her hand. He could hear his pulse pounding in his ears, his heart thumping against his ribs. Gripping the note, he leaned forward and spoke in a low harsh tone.

"Ms. Poste, this job isn't too much for you, is it? I know we're short staffed but with your habitual screw ups, I could hire a monkey and get better results."

She swallowed but said nothing, her face flushing a deeper red.

"You know that three of the criminal patients have escaped this month and the local police are already riding our collective hides about the only one they know about from *last* month. So please, if it's not too much," his voice began to rise until he shouted at the top of his lungs, "do your God damned job before I have you thrown out on your ass!"

Her bottom lip trembled but before she could make a sound, he whispered.

"If I see one tear escape those baby blues, I'll have you committed before you can say Bob's your uncle, understand?"

She bit her lip and nodded. He stared at her for half a minute as she struggled to keep her tears in check. Satisfied she'd been sufficiently cowed, he spun on his heel and marched down the hall toward his office. Dr. Black doubted Franks would be satisfied with more platitudes, his philosophies on controlled permissiveness and decentralization, or reminding him of the state laws requiring more patients' freedoms. He'd have to blow more smoke than a 200-acre forest fire up the chief's ass this time.

Passing the common room on his way, Dr. Black looked through the open door as sounds of a scuffle hit his ears. Two oversized patients, living embodiments of Tweedle Dee and Tweedle Dum, threw their fists against a diminutive patient, a thin rat-haired woman, who screeched with every punch. He could see dark bruises blooming across her petite arms, tears and snot mixed with the smears of blood from her nose and mouth, and he shook his head.

"Candy-ass harpy."

A jubilant shout from the other patients watching the spectacle floated out into the hall and Dr. Black chuckled.

The man wiped a wistful tear from his cheek and Marc stared at him, horrified. He thought the guy made everything up, maybe for shock value. But the more the man spoke, the more Marc believed the stories were true.

"I'm sure you're familiar with the hospital's history from

the 1980s on. The assaults and gross neglect; stealing from the patients' fund; the new superintendent being charged with more malpractice and rape lawsuits than you could shake your wiener at. You don't need me to bore you with the details."

Marc didn't realize he'd been guided to the empty building until they both stood outside the entrance. He stared up at the decrepit dormitory and saw a face in a second-floor window. A stringy haired man, emaciated and bloody in a sagging hospital gown, stared down at them. Marc scanned the remaining windows and saw dozens of men and women, patients and employees, all looking down at the two of them as they stood outside.

Marc's equipment lay just on the other side of the rusty and pitted door, but he was willing to leave it all behind if it meant he could get the hell out of here. The man's grip on his shoulders tightened and he choked on the fear clogging his throat.

"And now, this is all that remains of my beautiful hospital."

Marc shuddered but thought if he kept the man talking, he could distract the dude long enough to get away.

"You said you worked here. Were you an orderly or something, like right out of high school?"

"My dear boy, I created this place. I ran it until they forced me to retire."

Marc stared at him.

"But they built this place over sixty years ago. How could you...? You can't be. That's impossible."

The man smiled down at him as he reached forward to open the door, keeping Marc in a tight embrace. He raised an eyebrow, staring at Marc over the dark rims of his glasses.

"I look pretty snazzy for a dead man, eh?"

He shoved Marc into the dim hallway then slammed the door behind him. Marc slid down the wall, pulling his knees to his chest as Dr. Stephen Black studied the filming equipment. He set up the tripod and secured the digital camera on top.

"Marc, I can't allow my dream to be demolished. I thought the political and historical societies would talk in circles for eons, leaving my precious hospital alone. But it seems those boobs in Lansing finally got the ball rolling and so, here I am."

Dried leaves and trash rustled. Marc saw two men, dressed in white shirts and slacks, walking toward the camera. Dr. Black smiled.

"Ah, Gerald. Phil. Perfect timing. Our young friend here has been kind enough to provide this wonderful audio-visual equipment for us to record the reopening of MPH. Would you be so kind to get him in position?"

Gerald grabbed Marc by his shirt collar and hoisted him to his feet. Phil grabbed a worn cracked chair and placed it in front of the camera. Marc struggled in the former orderly's grip, but the man slammed him onto the chair. Marc's teeth clacked hard enough to send a jolt of pain up the side of his head. Gerald and Phil pressed down on Marc's shoulders preventing his escape. Dr. Black leaned down to look at the digital display. Marc sat alone in the rickety chair, swiveling his head back and forth to gawk at the empty space on either side of him.

"Perfect."

He pressed the record button then stood in front of the camera.

"Hello. My name is Dr. Stephen Black. I'm the creator of the state-of-the-art hospital you see before you. I know it's been closed for many a year but I'm about to change all that. This young man behind me is the first new patient in what I hope will be the dawn of a new era of mental health training and treatment. Join me on this exciting journey, won't you?"

He laughed, a long, loud, booming sound that roared through the empty hospital. A chorus of laughter rained down on all sides, pierced by the screams of the tormented and the damned. Gerald and Phil grabbed Marc under his arms and pulled him off the chair. Despite his thrashing, he couldn't break their hold. Dr. Black walked ahead, laughing and calling out to the long and forgotten dead.

"My friends and colleagues. Let us bring life back into this facility. Never again let history forget the MPH!"

On the camera display, alone and struggling against unseen captors, Marc was dragged down the hall and into the dark, as laughter echoed off the empty walls.

This story is based on Northville State Hospital (renamed Northville Regional Psychiatric Hospital in 1972). From what I understand, very little in the way of 'horror' happened there, at least in the beginning. With budget cuts and staff reductions, things spiraled into the world of nightmares, but nothing reported like what I've written. Well, almost nothing. I've taken liberties with newspaper clippings or went full-on hyperbole, playing the 'what if' game.

NSH was one of the few, or first, hospitals to use revolutionary treatments (music therapy, controlled permissiveness), encouraged public education on mental illness, secured patient representatives, etc., so please know I mean no disrespect at all. Now that the demolition of NSH has finally begun, I like to think the souls connected to the place have come to witness its destruction, and maybe find the peace they were denied in life.

Or maybe take some of us down with it.

RED ROVER

"**G**o on, get outta here!"

The man threw his arms in the air, frightening Danny into submission. He scuttled back onto the shore as the man hopped back in a small motorboat. The engine roared and puffed out black, oily smoke that scared Danny even more. He ran up toward the tree line to escape the loud noise and heady smell.

Soon, the man and his boat were small, dark shapes on the horizon. Danny didn't know why he was being left behind, all alone, but jumping into the icy water to swim after the man was not an option. The pull of the water was too strong, and could drown him in seconds.

Danny cried for hours on the beach but neither the man, nor anyone else, came for him. Before the sun set, he heard rustling in the greenery behind him. He spun around and saw three dark shapes push out of the deep cover, and walk onto the sand.

They approached Danny cautiously, the girl hanging back behind two husky guys. The scars crisscrossing their bodies, particularly their faces, alarmed Danny. He knew he couldn't be as tough as these two, having led a life of leisure for the past twenty-one years.

The one on the left moved forward, his blocky shoulders squared in challenge. The one on the right studied his companion, then imitated his posture. Danny stepped backward, not wanting a fight.

"Please," he cried. "I don't know what's happening."

The girl chuffed at the pair. "Back off. Let me talk to him."

They stepped to either side of her as she moved forward. She tilted her head to the side, studying Danny, and she almost smiled.

"How'd you get here?"

"My dad brought me in his boat."

"Did he say why he left you?"

"No! He's usually really noisy and chatty, but he didn't make any sound the whole ride over. I thought we were just having a good time, you know?"

She dipped her head in understanding. "Sounds like a lot of us here."

"Was it the same for you?"

She didn't answer, only raised her head to sniff the air, as if that were answer enough. "What are you called?"

"Danny. You?"

"Stella," she said as she tossed her head to either side. "That's Georgie and Tank."

Danny cocked his head, "Tank?"

The brute on the right growled. "Yeah, Tank. You got a problem with that?"

"No, no. No problem."

Stella smiled. "Don't worry about these guys. They're actually big softies."

Danny remained unsure, but Stella was definitely growing on him. She was nice, and smelled great.

"How long have you been here?" Danny asked.

"I can't remember exactly. But I can tell you I was the first one here."

He couldn't believe it. "You were left here all alone?"

"Yep. Georgie and Tank came next. Then before we knew it, there was a bunch of us."

Just then, the bushes behind the three of them rustled, and a whole group stepped out of the shadows. Some moved boldly with purpose, and others trembled with hunched shoulders and frightened eyes. Stella nodded at them, then addressed Danny again.

"There are a lot more, but we've formed our own crowds. *We're* all nice, but you'll have to watch out for the bunch on the other side of the woods."

Danny stared off to the left, beyond what seemed like a giant wall made of trees. He felt himself shake with fear, and he automatically inched toward Stella. She pressed herself against him.

"Stick with us, Danny, and you'll be okay."

A great howl ripped through the coming dark.

"What was that?" Danny asked as his shaking increased, and Stella rounded up the group.

"Time to go. We all know what they do after dark."

She looked at Danny and jerked her head toward the shelter of the foliage. "Come on, new guy."

He took one last look at the trees before jogging to catch up to Stella and the others.

Danny lost track of the time after a while. He stopped looking for his dad to return and tell him it was all a mistake. He learned to stay away from the woods, and never go anywhere alone on the island. In no time at all, he fell into sync with the others, each helping and protecting the rest. As long as they all stayed on their side, things went well.

Until that one night the group from beyond the trees broke through that unspoken but understood border, and infiltrated their peaceful grounds.

Danny and Stella had fallen asleep side by side. He didn't remember feeling this safe and happy before, not even with his dad. He was dreaming of the time he and the others ran along the beach, splashing and wrestling in the water, when Stella whined in his ear.

"Danny, wake up."

He was immediately awake and alert. "What's wrong?"

"They're close."

He didn't need Stella to explain. The Others had come into their territory. They'd been encroaching slowly, making random appearances at night. The last time, they snuck in and attacked Toby, the youngest and weakest among them. He survived, but with a mangled leg and fresh scars.

"You wake up the others. I'll hide with Toby," Danny said as he gave Stella a quick nudge. He slipped through the sleeping group. He found Toby snuggled up next to Tank. The big guy really was sweet and caring, especially with the smaller ones, like Toby.

"Toby? Wake up. We need to hide."

Toby stirred, scanned the area, and began to shiver. "I can smell them. Danny, I'm scared."

"I'll protect you. But we gotta go now."

"What's happening?" Tank asked as he shook himself awake, then stood, squaring his shoulders. "They're here. Where's Stella?"

Danny jerked his head to the right. "She's waking everyone else. I need to hide Toby."

Tank looked conflicted between running to Stella, and staying to protect his little friend. Toby moved next to Danny as he stared at Tank.

"Go. The group needs you. I'll be okay."

Tank paused for only a moment, then ran to find Stella. Toby looked up at Danny, still trembling.

"I'm sorry you got stuck having to watch me."

Danny gave Toby a soft push, careful not to knock him over. "I *want* to protect you, Toby. You're my friend. Come on, we gotta go."

Danny ambled beside Toby as he limped along. There was a mud hole close by so Toby could camouflage himself there. Since They had found him once, They might come looking for him again, figuring him an even easier target now with his damaged leg.

Once at the hole, Danny stood watch as Toby sunk into the muck, then fully submerged himself. His usual light hair was completely obscured by the black mud. When Danny thought Toby was well coated, he led his little friend to a grouping of heavily scented, flowering bushes. The shrubs would obscure them physically, and the flowers would help conceal both their scents from Them.

No sooner had they settled into their hiding place then three of Them rounded the corner and came into view, just a short distance away. Danny pulled Toby into an embrace, hoping to soothe his friend's quivering. They approached the bushes, stopping to scrutinize the immediate area, but soon moved farther down the beach.

When They we're far enough away, Toby relaxed and leaned against Danny. "Thanks."

"You're welcome."

They huddled together for a few more minutes, and Danny thought it might be safe to move. But an immense cry split the night, and he and Toby shook with fear. Not far off, the two friends could hear the ruckus of a huge fight begin between their group and the Others.

Screeches, cries, and screams of his friends and enemies echoed across the island. Danny stayed with Toby, despite his desire to join the fight. But he knew one more in the brawl probably wouldn't make much difference in its outcome.

After what felt like days, the fighting finally came to an end, and an eerie silence settled around them. He and Toby waited in the bushes until they knew they would be safe. When Stella finally came for them, Danny hardly recognized her. She was covered in sand and blood.

"Stella!"

Danny and Toby wriggled out from their hiding spot as Stella stood on shaky legs.

"Are you all right?" she asked.

"Us? We're fine. What about you? What happened?"

She shook herself, trying to knock off some of the grime, and blew out a sigh.

"They were more aggressive than ever before. Things must really be getting bad over there."

"What do you mean?"

"Resources," Toby squeaked.

Stella nodded, "That's my guess."

"What do you mean?" Danny asked again.

Stella jerked her head toward the beach. "Follow me. I'll show you."

The three of them walked down to the shore. Dozens of dark shapes dotted the beach, a few right at the water's edge. The incoming tide was already trying to claim them for the sea.

Danny approached one and cried out when he recognized Tank, though just barely. Part of his face had been chewed off, one of his legs was missing, and several ribs poked through the ragged and torn flesh of his chest.

Stella and Toby moved next to Danny, and stared down at their dead friend.

"Food, Danny. They're running out of food," Stella said.

Toby whimpered with grief as Stella stood over Tank's body. The horror finally registered and Danny turned away to retch. The rest of the group wandered over, huddling for warmth and security, in the crisp air coming off the water. When Danny finished, he stood with the others.

"What do we do now?"

"We let the sea take them. We'll keep watch, just to be sure They don't come back for more, or to finish off what they left behind."

"Then what?"

Stella turned to look at him. "Then, Danny, we try to survive."

What remained of the group stood in the sand, watching and waiting for the tide to come in and swallow their brethren. By the time the first orange hints of morning colored the horizon, all the bodies were gone. Most of them cried during the night, but now all were quiet as they left the beach to find some much-needed sleep.

Stella was the last to leave, standing watch over the waves as they receded. Danny moved next to her, nudging her shoulder.

"You all right, Stella?"

"Honestly, I'm scared, Danny,"

"Of Them?"

"No. Of becoming Them."

"Why would you even think that?"

She turned to look at him. "Think about it. We're on a small piece of land, surrounded by water, no way off. And though we've been rationing food, it won't last forever. Eventually, we're gonna run out and..."

She left her thought unfinished and stared back out at the water. Danny shook with fear at the thought. Though this group was pretty close, protecting each other, comforting one another when they got scared or lonely, when the time came for survival over friendship, which would endure?

After that night, the cliques began to drift apart. Alliances were broken and reformed, trust was lost, and allies abandoned. Despite his efforts, Danny only retained Stella and Toby as close friends. And Toby only lasted until the next full moon before Steve, a once close and trusted friend, attacked and ate the little guy.

There was no more 'Us' and 'Them'. All of them had become animals, desperate to survive another day.

As their numbers dwindled—all their numbers—Danny feared no one would even live long enough to see the rains return. Though most of his friends hated getting wet, Danny always loved it. His dad would get so angry when Danny ran around outside for hours in the rain. But when he could finally be coaxed to go back inside the house, his dad would laugh and dry him off, then give him a bowl of something hot to warm him up.

Danny hadn't thought about his dad for a while. He wondered what he was up to, if he was okay, but mostly he felt sad and angry. If he ever saw his dad again, what would he do? What would he say to the man who abandoned him in this hell?

The morning after Toby was taken, Danny and Stella lounged under a copse of trees, delaying the need to get up as long as possible. Partly because there was nothing to eat, but also to reduce their exposure to the others trolling for prey.

Their lazy morning was interrupted by a loud, growling noise, coming from the beach. They stared at each other for a few moments. Danny cocked his head.

"That sounds like a boat, like what my dad used to bring me here."

"Let's go look."

They poked their heads out from the shade of the trees, and spotted a few of the others doing the same. No one seemed brave enough to approach, except Stella. She warily walked toward the water, and Danny followed close behind.

Chuck Parker, the director of the Michigan chapter of the Wildlife Refuge Organization, maneuvered a motorboat toward the shore of Garden Island, an uninhabited small landmass in northern Lake Michigan. After receiving some disturbing information regarding local animal activity, the director gathered a small group of volunteers to investigate.

Now, as the craft arrived at the beach, the motor gunned loudly before Chuck cut it off. The others jumped out and pulled the boat onto the sand, securing it to the shore to keep it from floating away.

"Okay everyone, gather up," Chuck said to the volunteers. "Just a reminder—don't approach any animals you see. We don't know what condition they're in, or if they're rabid or what, okay?"

Four of the volunteers nodded, murmuring to each other. But Katie was looking up the beach and pointing.

"Look!"

Two emaciated dogs, their bones practically piercing their skin and patchy fur, walked slowly toward them. The male remained slightly behind the female, but both seemed more curious than vicious.

"Jesus," Chuck breathed. "Look at those poor things. What the hell were their owners thinking?"

He moved forward, holding out his hands. "Hey there. I'm not gonna hurt you. It's okay."

He knelt down and let the dogs approach him. The female

extended her neck to sniff his hands, then looked at the male behind her. She chuffed at him and he stepped up, also sniffing the director.

Chuck smiled and gave the male dog a little scratch under his chin. The poor creature pressed against Chuck's hand, and the man nearly burst into tears.

"That's a good boy. What's your name, huh?" Chuck adjusted the dog's collar and looked at the dirty tag hanging from it. "Danny. Is that your name, boy?"

When he spoke the dog's name, Danny wagged his tail and offered a quiet bark. The female moved closer, still sniffing, but less cautious. The other volunteers gathered behind Chuck as he pet the two starving animals

"Katie, grab some jerky for these two."

Katie ran to the boat and pulled out a plastic bag filled with dried beef. She handed the whole thing to Chuck. The dogs immediately pushed their noses against it, then tried to eat the bag.

Chuck laughed, "Whoa, whoa. Don't worry. You'll both get some."

He pulled out two small pieces, one for each dog, and offered it to them. The female snapped at it so hard, she bit Chuck's fingers. He tried not to overreact, which could scare either of them off.

"Hey, leave some fingers, sweetie."

She licked her chops, then turned to look behind her. Dozens and dozens of dogs, all starving, moved out of the cover of the trees and onto the beach. The female barked at them, and they all began to trot forward.

"Uh..." was all Chuck could manage before Danny grabbed the bag and took it to the approaching animals. The dogs swarmed over the jerky, devouring it in under a minute. As they did, more dogs came out of the trees.

"Uh..." Katie mimicked Chuck, but the other volunteers seemed unfazed by the advancing pack of starving dogs. They moved slowly forward to greet the animals, each carrying some food provisions.

"Oh, look how many there are."

"The poor things!"

"Good thing we brought a lot of food."

The original two dogs remained next to Chuck and Katie, as if waiting to see how the rest of the pack would react. The volunteers were quickly overwhelmed. The pack took the offered food and devoured it all in minutes.

But it wasn't enough for the large group of animals that had been abandoned on this tiny spit of land where they'd been left to starve. The majority of them fell upon the volunteers, snarling and spitting. Their screams echoed across the beach.

A small cluster, though, broke off and inched toward Chuck and Katie.

"Katie, don't panic. And don't run. Just get up as slowly as possible and walk to the boat."

"But—"

"Just do it."

They rose an inch at a time, but before they could take one step, the two original dogs moved behind them, blocking their retreat. The male snarled and the female snapped twice. Chuck and Katie swiveled their heads back and forth, trying to keep an eye on the approaching dogs and the two animals behind them.

The female lunged, biting into Katie's hand. The woman screamed in pain and terror. The male gripped Chuck's ankle in his teeth. Both volunteers went down, and the advancing pack ran forward to join the feast.

. . .

Three days later, another motorboat with six employees of the WRO bounced on the waves as it approached the small island. The team leader, Randy, shouted over the cacophony of the rushing water and grumbling engine.

"We haven't heard from the initial reconnaissance group for three days. We don't know what happened and don't know what we'll find out here today. But we'll keep sending as many people as necessary to learn the truth!"

The small boat pulled up to shore and two people jumped out, mooring it in the sand. As the others discussed rescue plans, a pack of dogs watched them from the tree line, each licking their chops in anticipation.

Back in 2009, many citizens of Malaysia decided that two empty islands offshore would be the perfect place to dump their unwanted dogs–because they bit people, or pooped too much (yes, that was an excuse given), or they couldn't handle them for one reason or another. They ASSUMED the natural resources of the islands would sustain the animals, not considering the finite food situation for 300+ dogs. When the Selangor Society of Prevention of Cruelty to Animals finally arrived on the islands, some of the dogs had turned to cannibalism to survive. Personally, I think the way my story ends is more poetic than the truth, but sadly, there's very little information on the status of those animals today, despite efforts of SPCA workers to rescue them.

His grandmother's death came as a shock. Apparently sitting on your front porch, minding your own business, meant your doom in this family. John sat in his grandmother's living room, rifling through a trunk of old papers and photos, while his mom boxed up the accumulated knick knacks and tchotchkes from the past seventy-five years. He flipped through a worn photo album and landed on a page that held a large, single photo, black and white and a little fuzzy. He held it up.

"Hey, mom. Who are all these people?"

His mother held a small dish in her hand, half wrapped with brown paper, as she looked at the photo.

"Oh, my. That was a family reunion, long before you were born. Long before I was born, for that matter."

"No shit?"

"Johnathan, please don't cuss."

"Sorry. I didn't know they had cameras when the dinosaurs roamed the earth."

"That joke *never* gets old, my dear."

He chuckled. "Sorry again. But seriously, is grandma in here?"

His mom put down the dish, then sat beside him on the saggy couch. Why his grandma hadn't pitched this dilapidated piece of crap, John could never figure out. The cushions sunk deeper into the springs, and his mother winced.

"I wish your grandmother had replaced this damn thing years ago."

"Mother, *language*."

She smirked at him then leaned over to study the photograph. She tapped the image of a young girl, sitting in the front row with a dozen other kids.

"That's grandma. She was probably ten or so in this photo, so that would make it around 1943, give or take a year."

His mom traced the edge of the plastic sheet covering the photo and pulled up the corner. She released the picture from the remains of the tacky coating that held it in place. She turned it over, and read the faded scribble on the back.

"September 13, 1942. Jarvis Homestead, Family Reunion. Gaylord, MI."

"That's a lot of people for one family."

His mother laughed. "Different times back then. Your great-grandfather couldn't fight in the war. Polio left him half crippled."

"That didn't seem to stop his ability to populate the entire county with Jarvis babies."

She laughed again, a great belly laugh that made John smile. He worried his mom might never laugh again after grandma died.

"You're not wrong. I think they ended up with fourteen children at one count, your grandma being the second to last."

John tapped the photograph as he counted. "I only see twelve whippersnappers though. And grandma looks to be the youngest."

His mother's smiled faded as she sighed. "Different times back then, John."

She patted his knee then went back to wrapping knick knacks. He bit his lip. Just when his mom started to get the life back in her cheeks, he had to ruin it. He traced his fingers over his grandma's smiling face, the cheeks round like a chipmunk hoarding acorns. He recognized a handful of other family members, great aunts and uncles, but the rest remained a mystery. One face in particular, one that looked even more out of focus than the rest, made him stop. John brought the picture closer, though the blurred image didn't sharpen in any way. The man stood off to the side, almost like an afterthought. His clothes matched the rest of the men of the time, though the sweater vest worn over the long-sleeved button-down shirt dressed up the otherwise casual style for the event. His aviator sunglasses reflected the bright sun; the little hair he had sat flat against a balding pate; high-waisted slacks accentuated his thin frame, the sharp crease hanging just above two-toned Oxford shoes.

Probably one of the most innocuous looking people John had ever seen. So why did he make John feel so uneasy?

"Hey, mom. Who's this guy?"

He put the album on the couch, and took the picture to her. She examined it.

"Who?"

"This guy."

His mother bent forward to study the man, but she shook her head.

"I don't know. He doesn't look like part of the family, does he?"

"Not really. Maybe he's a great-great uncle or something."

He saw his mother shake with an involuntary tremble. "Maybe. He gives me the shivers, though."

John didn't want to agree with her, as it might dampen her mood further. He shrugged and put the picture back on top of the album.

"Well, there were *a lot* of people in that family..."

His mom giggled, and he gave her shoulder a squeeze. "I'll save the photos and miscellany for later. Want me to go through grandma's room?"

The relief on her face almost made John cry. "Would you, honey? I...I don't think I can handle that right now. Maybe just organize her things?"

"You got it."

He kissed her on the nose then moved to the back of the house, into grandma's bedroom. The late afternoon sun shone through the white frilly curtains that had hung in this room as long as John could remember. The rose wallpaper and accent pillows brightened the room further, which fit so well with his grandmother's personality. But the hulking wooden wardrobe on the far side of the room darkened the cheery mood every time.

Made of thick oak, it had been stained dark brown, almost black. The designs carved into the front of it, along the sides, and over the doors, imparted no evil vibes on their own. But when taken as a whole, like one giant collage, it gave John the shivers. Dozens of cherubs mingled with skeletal figures; musical instruments and weapons of war stacked in giant piles at each bottom corner; a shining sun hovered above storm clouds and bolts of lightning. And in the middle, a lone figure split in two, decorated both doors.

It looked like any random middle-aged man you'd run into at the grocery store. His clothing bore elements of modern and vintage styles. The wood grain around him radiated outward, in contrast to the natural grain, giving him a haloed effect. And he held in his hands a sideways hourglass. When the doors stood open, the hourglass broke in half at the narrow neck, and John expected to see a little pile of sand spill on to the floor whenever he opened the damn thing.

"The 13th Man."

John turned. If he didn't know better, he would have thought his grandma whispered in his ear, instead of her remembered voice that popped into his head. He talked with his grandma a lot about this wardrobe over the years. He always thought she brought it up because she knew it spooked him so much. But their most recent conversation popped into his head, when she'd revealed so much about its history. Almost like she knew she'd be dead soon, and needed to pass the information on to another generation.

"That's the 13th Man."

"Who is, grandma?"

She pointed a knobby finger toward the giant wardrobe while she rocked in her chair in the corner of her room. John had a skein of yarn stretched over his hands while she knitted her latest Christmas gift. The scene was almost Norman Rockwell in its normalcy, but the topic of conversation was anything but all American. John turned his head to look at it.

"The guy in the middle?"

"Yes. He's the owner."

John could feel his confused expression. "What's that supposed to mean?"

His grandmother smiled as she continued working, the knitting needles clacking every few seconds. But he could tell she wasn't looking at the shawl; she was reminiscing about the past.

"My grandmother had the wardrobe before me. And her grandmother before her. I can't remember exactly why, but it's

passed down to every other generation, grandmother to granddaughter."

She glanced up at John, and winked. *"Though I suppose it'll be yours when I die, John, as none of my children wanted to have any girls."*

John laughed. *"I always thought that was kinda weird."*

She shrugged. *"Maybe it was the universe trying to tell us something."*

"Like what?"

"Like it was time to stop."

"Stop what?"

She paused her knitting to look up at the 13th Man, and sighed. *"Perhaps our obligations have been met, and he can go on to another family now."*

John looked back at the wardrobe again as his grandmother spoke. *"Lord knows we've paid our dues, and then some."*

"Grandma, you're not making any sense, but you're already creeping the bejeesus out of me."

She laughed, a soft melodic giggle, then tugged on the yarn to get his attention. He stared at her, smiling. But the fierce gaze she held, her eyes bright and her cheeks red, forced his smile to sag into a grimace of discomfort. Her hushed voice, an urgent whisper, made the hair on his arms stand up.

"It's up to you now, John. You need to get rid of it. I'll tell you everything you need to know, but get it away from this family. It can have someone else's now."

Before she could continue, John's mom came to the house, shouting her arrival. *"Hey, folks. I'm here. And I've brought dinner!"*

John and his grandmother stared at each other. Her mouth hung open, unspoken words stuck at the back of her throat. She sighed, then put down her knitting. She took the yarn he'd been holding, and put it on top of the unfinished shawl.

"It's all right, John. We can talk later."

But they never did. They ate dinner together that night, sat on the back porch, and talked about old times. After his mom left, John gave his grandma a hug, smiling against her ear.

"I'll come over tomorrow, okay? You can get back to that shawl, and tell me everything you know about the 13th Man. Sound good?"

She leaned back from his embrace. A soft smile curled her lips, but her eyes filled with unspilled tears. She caressed his face with a thin, cold hand that felt soft as silk.

"All right, dear. Tomorrow."

He opened his mouth to ask if she was all right, but she'd already stepped back, her hand resting on the edge of the open door. He nodded.

"See you tomorrow."

If he'd even entertained the idea she could be dead by morning, John would have insisted on staying, and talking all through the night. But he assumed they'd have more time, and went home.

When she didn't answer his calls the next day, he drove to her house. She didn't answer the door either. He had the spare keys, and let himself inside. Nothing looked or felt out of place. He called out to her as he searched the house before finding her sitting on the edge of her bed, in front of the wardrobe.

"Grandma, why didn't you answer me?"

He moved through the room to face her. "Grandma—?"

She wore the same clothes as the previous night, though at some point she'd slipped off her shoes. A cold cup of tea sat on the dresser, as if waiting for her to enjoy it before going to sleep. Her head sagged forward, but he could still see her face. Her open eyes stared at the wardrobe.

And the 13th Man.

The doors stood open an inch, the hourglass split in half.

Automatically, John looked down at the floor, expecting to see that little pile of sand that never appeared. The wardrobe itself seemed as normal as ever, though the broken hourglass was a bit ham-fisted even in its timeliness.

That was the last he'd thought of the cabinet until now. He stood before it and sighed. He opened its doors, the hinges creaking loudly, and stared at the assortment of clothes hanging on the left. On the right sat four drawers, each holding a variety of undergarments and clothing accessories, none of which John looked forward to rifling through for donation or the trash.

He threw the dresses, slacks, and blouses on the bed. He bent to retrieve the four pairs of shoes, and a small bundle fell out of a black loafer. It clunked against the wood and came to rest on the carpet. He put the shoes to the side, and picked up the object.

A yellowed lace handkerchief had been knotted around a small, hard item. He freed it after a minute of struggle—a small, silver key. John scratched his head, and gazed around the room. No immediate answer revealed itself to where this key belonged, so he searched the drawers inside the wardrobe.

Grimacing, he dug through the top two which held his grandma's underwear. The last thing he wanted to do was handle granny panties, but after quickly pushing the items around, he found nothing aside from a new appreciation for his grandma's conservative style choices.

Nothing odd hid among her socks and hosiery in the third drawer. In the fourth drawer, behind a conglomeration of mismatched jewelry, loose hair pins, a few small scarves, more handkerchiefs, a lone leather belt, and a tuna can holding dozens of buttons, John found a small, locked box. He eased it out of its hiding place, and studied it in the faint light coming through the window.

The plain box possessed no designs or sigils on its surface. The simple domed lid revealed no sinister secrets. The aged edges and corners indicated a much loved, albeit ordinary, trinket. The escutcheon plate surrounding the keyhole, however, told a different story.

The intricate filigree, swirls and loops engraved into the silver, hypnotized John. He stared at them for several long minutes, tracing a finger over the unending twists and turns of the design. It wasn't until the lock snapped open that he realized he'd taken the key, put it in the keyhole, and opened the box.

Shaking his head to clear it, he focused on the curio. He pulled up the lid, excited and terrified to see what it held. And like the box itself, the contents appeared mundane. A thin stack of cards, a few small black and white photographs, newspaper clippings, and some loose coins.

"Not exactly what I expected, but okay."

He sat on the bed, and dumped the contents out onto the rose print comforter. He picked up the coins, and tossed them up and down in his hand. They looked ordinary, but on closer inspection, he noted the faces or symbols on some of them: a profile of Lady Liberty on one cent; a seated woman on a silver twenty-cent coin; a crescent moon next to the roman numeral three; a copper half cent; a corroded coin with the letters 'VOC' stamped on it; the rest with varying figures and symbols he recognized from the change in his own pockets.

Then he noted some of the minted dates: 1994, 1890, 1942, 1903.

"What the hell?"

He put the coins aside then inspected the pictures and clippings. The articles covered a multitude of dates, but the subject of each revolved around death. Accidents, sickness, unexplained phenomena, pandemics, and even a few homicides. He recognized his mom's maiden name, Lansing, in several articles. His grandma's maiden name, Jarvis, popped up in a few of the articles as well, some dating back to the 1800s.

The photographs consisted of family portraits and social gatherings, the earliest from the mid-nineteenth century. And in each photo, two people had been circled—one in black ink, and another in red. The black marked various relatives, men, women, and children of all different ages, none of whom he recognized. But the red ink...

John lined up all the pictures. One man had been circled in red in every photo. His clothing changed in each era, but John harbored no doubt that the thinning hair, the slim build, and the blurred facial features belonged to the same guy. John grabbed the sixth picture from the end, the same family photo from the album in the living room.

But in this copy, the man had been circled in red, and a teenager circled in black. John scrabbled through the articles again, and found one from 1942. The headline read, "John Jarvis, 14, dies in freak railroad accident in Mackinac City." John remembered his mom named him after her uncle, but she never spoke about his death.

John lined up the news clippings, and discovered each one matched a date on one of the pictures. None of the photographs or articles dated earlier than 1851. He then grabbed the coins, and matched *those* with the articles and photographs. Putting them in chronological order, each set ranged in dates from 1851 to 1994, in thirteen-year increments.

"Holy shit."

He grabbed the cards. A solid red block of color decorated the backs, and an image of a robed skeleton stared back at him from the front. The old and worn tarot card had tattered edges and bent corners. He removed the rubber band securing the pack, and fanned the cards across the bed.

The collection held a dozen of the Major Arcana of Death. Different art styles, imagery, time periods, colors, and designs. His grandma had only collected Death cards. But why?

He noted every card had a Roman numeral somewhere in their designs. Usually at the top or bottom, the letters "X-I-I-I" would be in bold print or a different color, making it stand out from the rest of the artwork.

"Thirteen. Is this...?"

He grabbed his phone, and opened the search engine installed. After a few minutes of scrolling, he found an article about the Tarot card of Death.

- Death is the 13th trump, or Major Arcana, card in most traditional Tarot decks. While frightening to most, the Death card often means change or transformation, not necessarily physical death. It signifies the end of one phase, and the beginning of another.

While that did make John feel a bit better, as he poked at the cards again, a small laminated slip of paper appeared from behind one of them. He didn't recognize the handwriting, but the date written in the upper corner shocked him: 1851. He lifted the note closer to read it.

Now it begins. If what the old woman said is true, once thirteen have been collected, from each of the Promised Years, we may break this wretched tether it has latched to our family. Once gathered, they must be destroyed by flame—the cards and the cursed wardrobe. These instructions must be passed down until the 13th Man has taken his final sacrifice. Only then can this madness end. May God be with us, and our future.

It was signed Maybell Jarvis.

John dropped the note, and studied the Death cards. Each one had a year scribbled on the front that matched one of the sets before him, twelve in total, the last one from 1994. If they needed to collect thirteen, it meant the next sequential year hadn't been accounted for yet. He grabbed the little box, and upended it. A lone penny tumbled out, bright and shiny and new.

He slowly looked over at the wardrobe. Though he knew he'd closed the doors, they hung open an inch, just enough to break the hourglass design.

John watched the wardrobe as he began collecting all the items on the bed to put back into the box. With each hand movement, the doors opened another half inch. By the time he'd gathered everything and locked them away, the doors stood wide open. He jumped off the bed, pressing his back against the far wall, and clutched the keepsake to his chest.

The wardrobe didn't want to be destroyed. It didn't want to leave his family. Too bad for the 13th Man because John wasn't going to let him feed off any more family misfortune, not if he could help it.

The issue now was getting his mom out of here so he could return alone, burn the cards and that damned wardrobe, and break the curse. John left the bedroom, carrying the small box, and sat on the couch in the living room. He sighed loudly while glancing at his mom. She put down the figurine she'd been wrapping, and sat next to him.

"What's that, hon?"

"Just a little box of junk grandma and I used to collect. Old coins, buttons, that kind of thing. I'd forgotten all about it."

She wrapped her arm around his shoulders, and squeezed. "Need to take a break?"

He nodded. "Why don't we both take a break? I'll drive you home, we'll get some takeout, then come back tonight. Maybe even tomorrow?"

"Of course, John. Honestly, I was starting to feel a little overwhelmed myself."

He stood, tucking the box under one arm, and offered a hand to his mom. "So what do you think, Chinese? Mexican?"

She tilted her head forward, staring at him from under her bangs, and offering a smirk. He laughed.

"Pizza it is."

As she grabbed her purse, John glanced back at the bedroom. He thought he heard the faint squeak of a door hinge. He rushed himself and his mother out the front door before she heard it, too.

They shared memories of his grandmother, punctuated with a lot of laughter and tears, over pizza and beer. John convinced his mom they could wait until morning to finish packing up the house. She agreed, and he hoped his relief didn't show. He grabbed his keys, and gave her a soft kiss on the cheek before leaving.

"Want me to pick you up tomorrow?"

"That would be wonderful, thanks."

"See you then. Love you."

"Love you too, sweetie."

John drove back to his grandma's house. Once there, he sat

in the driveway, his car's interior light shining as he reread the note from Maybell. He knew his grandma had gasoline in the garage, and a vase filled with matchbooks in the kitchen. He just needed to figure out how to get that cumbersome wardrobe from the bedroom to the back yard.

John clutched the box as he entered his grandma's house. He didn't like being here alone, at night, with that thing. He eyed the door to the bedroom as he moved into the kitchen. Grabbing the pen and notepad by the phone, he sat at the table. He needed to make a record of tonight's events, just like Maybell did over 150 years ago. If everything went well, he could rip it up later. If not...at least he'd have left a clue for anyone unlucky enough to face the same horror in the future.

I don't know if my plan will work. All I have to go on is a handwritten note from 1851 that explains what to do to break the curse that's been linked to this family for generations. I'm going to burn the wardrobe and the cards tonight. If all goes well, my family should be free. If not, I hope God or the universe or whatever high power is out there can help the next person succeed where I failed.

He read it over. Something told him to keep the note cryptic, to not divulge too many details. As if researching the curse amplified the power needed to break it. He hoped that was true. He put his and Maybell's notes in the box, along with the coins, photos, and articles. John also grabbed the 1942 family photo he and his mom looked at earlier today and, finding a red marker next to the phone, circled the 13th Man, then stuffed it inside before locking it. He knotted the key in the handkerchief, then put it and the locked box in one of the cardboard packing boxes in the living room.

Taking a deep breath, he headed into the bedroom, gripping the tarot cards in his hand. The wardrobe sat on the far wall, just where he'd left it, the doors closed. The 13th Man seemed so ordinary now, neither threatening nor dangerous. Maybe John didn't have to destroy it after all.

Dizziness blurred his vision, and he collapsed onto the bed. He shook his head, realizing the 13th Man was trying to stop him, filling his mind with notions of safety. He glared up at him.

"No way, pal. You're history as of tonight."

After stuffing the cards into his back pocket, John wrenched the doors open, and secured his hands inside. With a heave, the wardrobe slid away from the wall. It felt lighter than he'd expected, and gave him little resistance as he pulled and tugged and pushed it out of the bedroom, down the hall, through the kitchen, and onto the back porch.

He struggled a moment as he guided it down the three steps to the patio. When he thought he'd wedged it against the door frame, the entire wardrobe tipped forward, and crashed onto the cement. Surprisingly, it didn't break, and only suffered minimal scratching on one side.

He wished it had broken apart, but John supposed not everything would go smoothly before the night was out. He ran back inside to grab the matches from the kitchen, then ransacked his grandma's garage for the full gas can, finding a small hatchet in the process.

John spend the next hour chopping the wardrobe into kindling. But no matter how many times he brought the hatchet down on the doors, the 13th Man wouldn't break. Even the varnish refused to chip. It didn't matter. It would still go up in flames with the rest of it.

He grabbed the cards from his pocket, and tossed them on

top of the splintered wardrobe. They fluttered in the air, and landed in a perfect circle around the 13th Man. John swallowed, doubt beginning to invade his thoughts. He shook his head, ridding himself of the 13th Man's influence.

Picking up the gas can, he emptied its contents over the piled wood. He coughed as the fumes rose, waving them away as much as possible, before tossing the can aside. Satisfied he'd used enough of the accelerant, he grabbed the matches. Standing over the ruined cabinet, John struck a match then set the entire book aflame.

"Go to Hell, asshole. You're done with this family."

He dropped it, and the fumes ignited. John leaned away from the conflagration, raising a hand to protect his face from the building heat. Against his better judgement, however, he moved *toward* the bonfire. He needed to see the wardrobe destroyed, all the way down to ash, before he could relax.

As he approached the fire, he saw the tarot cards curl and whither into nothing, but the wood didn't burn. Though the flames climbed, nearly as tall as John, the wood itself remained untouched. The figure of the 13th Man sat between the doors, the dark varnish reflecting the orange light of the fire.

Suddenly, he shifted. John rubbed his eyes, and looked again. The 13th Man stared at him.

"What the hell?"

The form pulled away from the doors, not split down the middle, but a full and complete body. It stood, the wood creaking as it straightened to its full height. John stumbled back, and fell on his ass, scraping his palms on the concrete patio. The 13th Man stepped toward him, his hands reaching, almost in a gesture of peace.

"This can't be happening."

"I'm afraid it is, John."

The figure smiled as it stood over him. "I'm not going to

hurt you. I want to thank you for freeing me."

"What?"

The 13th Man chuckled. "I'm afraid the sorceress didn't tell Maybell the whole truth. Yes, if she set fire to the cards and the wardrobe, it would break my connection to the family. But, as with any affliction, there's always a catch with the cure."

John tried to scuttle backward, but the man was on him in seconds, straddling his legs with the pressure of solid oak.

"I *will* leave, John. But the one who tries to break the curse has to take my place. In this case, you."

He poked John in the chest with a thick wooden finger.

"Your family will never be free, John. That's why it's called a curse."

The 13th Man tilted his head back and laughed with the deep echo of a hollow log. A rumble and crack boomed, and the man looked behind him. His grin widened as he turned back to John.

"It's time for you to go now, John."

The 13th Man yanked John to his feet then pushed him toward the wardrobe, doorless but otherwise intact. John felt a wooden hand urge him forward. With each step, the pressure at his back softened, and when he arrived at the wooden monstrosity, John spun around.

The man from the 1942 photograph, balding, bespectacled, banal, smiled back at him. He gripped the front of John's shirt, and lifted him off the ground.

"Goodbye, John. And thank you."

The 13th Man extended his arms and pushed. John crashed into the back panel of the wardrobe. He scrabbled forward, but couldn't escape. The doors floated to either side of him, Horrified, he watched them undulate, like heat waves on black top, as they molded to his body. He stiffened, his tissues morphing to match the oak of the wardrobe. As his vision darkened, as the doors settled into place—and his body with them—the former 13th Man offered a curt nod before striding down the driveway, and out of sight.

John tried to scream, but only the sound of the locking doors could be heard as darkness enveloped him, and the new cycle began.

Marie sat on the back porch with her nephew. The low sun lit the sky with an orange fire, and the crisp September air rushed through the open windows. She put her teacup back on its saucer, and turned to him.

"So, Lindsey's due soon, right?"

"Three weeks. I can't believe how quickly it's gone by."

Marie laughed. "For you, maybe. I bet Lindsey's been ready for a while."

"True."

"Do you pick a name?"

"We decided on Ruby, since this would have been her first granddaughter."

"Oh, Charlie, that's wonderful. I'm sure mom would have liked that."

"We thought so, too."

"I guess that means the wardrobe can finally go to another girl."

"That would be great. We need some extra storage for all the baby stuff."

"I bet. I think John would have approved, too."

Charlie stared at his aunt, and she laughed.

"Don't give me that look."

"What?"

"That 'sad puppy dog' look. I'm fine, really."

"I still miss him."

"So do I, sweetie. I can't believe it's been thirteen years."

"How could he just leave? What was he thinking?"

Marie didn't answer.

"I'm sorry. I didn't mean—"

"Don't worry about it. I really am okay."

He nodded then stood. "Well, I hate to throw a wet blanket on our nice afternoon and leave, but Lindsey's waiting."

"If you two need anything, don't hesitate to call, all right?"

"Love you, Aunt Marie."

"Love you, too, Charlie."

Marie waved as he backed out of the driveway. When he'd gone, she went inside, gathered up her dishes, and put them in the sink. She felt drained, an exhaustion that hit her every evening since John had disappeared. Her only comfort was sitting next to her mom's wardrobe for a few hours before going to sleep. She didn't know why, but the carving on it reminded her of John. She couldn't remember if it always looked that way, or if she was just projecting.

She sat on the edge of her bed across from the wardrobe, and smiled at it.

"Looks like we're finally going to be able to pass you along to mom's first granddaughter."

Marie's vision blurred as tears filled her eyes. She wiped them away angrily, then laughed.

"This is a good thing. Maybe keeping you here stops me from moving on, you know?"

It didn't answer, and Marie didn't hold back the sobs that wracked her body. She pressed her face into her hands, crying for her son, for the answers she would never get, and for the new loss she would suffer once the wardrobe left her possession. She let the fresh wave of sadness wash over her as she laid back on the bed, and wept.

The eyes of the 13th Man glistened in the fading light.

SEEP

"Stop fighting me, boy. This is the only way to save the family, and you know it."

"Pa, please. Don't—"

Arthur pulled his son along by the scruff of his collar. Daniel kicked and dragged his feet, flailing his arms behind him, trying to dislodge his father's grip. But his father had two feet of height and at least 100 pounds weight over Daniel, so his struggles accomplished nothing. He twisted around and saw his mother standing at the foot of the stairs. The twins, Myrtle and Marie, clung to her skirts as tears streaked down their dirty cheeks. The scars where their ears used to be burned deep red from their crying. Maddie peeked out from behind his mother's hip, clutching the worn apron tied there this morning.

Francis sat on the steps behind them all, his tremors more vicious than ever, nearly knocking the boy from his precarious perch. His remaining leg kicked out suddenly, striking Maddie's knee, but the older girl never flinched. She'd been giggling into her closed fist during the whole commotion, then suddenly burst into a fit of sobbing.

Arthur reached the door then turned to speak to his wife.

"Grace, get control of that girl, and take Francis back upstairs before he hurts himself."

She nodded and corralled the children upstairs to the bedroom they all shared. Grace offered one last, sorrowful look at her oldest boy before resuming her task.

"Ma."

Daniel called out to her, but she never looked at him again. The last he saw of her were the limp strands of hair clinging to her sweaty brow as she and his siblings disappeared from his sight. Any fight remaining in him drained along with his expectation for survival. He sagged in his father's hands, and offered no further resistance. His father clasped his shoulder, not as his executioner, but as a father.

"I knew you'd come to understand, son. Thank you."

The two of them left the house and trudged down the dirt path leading from the front door to the back yard and, eventually, the homestead's well. The morning sky cast a dreary pall over their surroundings, presenting a muted haze that dulled the details of even the largest evergreens. The daisies at the corner of the house drooped with the burden of a faded, lifeless yellow; the grass laid flat, as if bowing down to the mediocrity of the grey sky; even the apple tree cried its late spring blooms in a shower of ashy pink.

The dark stone well squatted only a few yards from the house. The headstones of his grandparents and two uncles sat as sentries on either side of the structure, their graves having been moved from the back of the property last year. Though only twelve, Daniel's head told him that burying dead bodies nearer to their water source only made matters worse, not better, but he had no power to change the tide of the community's laws and traditions, nor his father's hand.

And now, with his father's resolve firm and unchangeable, Daniel quietly accepted his fate. He stood, shoulders slumped and spirit broken, as his father removed the wooden cover from the well. Arthur stared down into its depth. The scowl furrowing his brow had more to do with the reduced water level than having to imprison his son within the dark pit.

"The water is as low as I've ever seen it. It won't be as quick as I would like."

"For who?"

"What?"

Daniel stared up at his father. "Your family's recovery, or your son's death. Which one do you want most, Pa?"

Arthur strode around the low wall of the well and struck Daniel across the face. The boy crumpled to the ground, but refused to cry.

"How dare you talk back to me. Are you so selfish that you won't do anything to save us? What about your mother? Your sisters? Take Francis. You've seen how ill he's become. You're the only one who isn't sick with this new plague, so only your essence can save us."

Daniel placed a hand against his cheek as he grinned up at his murderer. "Paint it any color you like, Pa. You're killing me, and my death won't save anyone before this is all over."

His father hesitated, almost as if Daniel's words convinced him to question the sanity of his actions. A small spark of hope ignited in his chest as his father knelt down and, in an uncharacteristic manner, caressed Daniel's cheek. They each offered the other a smile, but before Daniel could clasp his father's hand in his own, Arthur grabbed his son under his arms, hoisted him aloft, and threw him into the well.

The day came to an abrupt end as darkness swallowed Daniel whole.

When Daniel returned to consciousness, his mind focused on two issues: one, his left shoulder burned with searing pain, and two, his entire body shivered with cold as he lay submerged in half a foot of water. He choked as some slipped over his mouth and nose. Forcing himself upright sent fresh fiery pain through his shoulder and chest, and he began to cry.

Though he knew no help would come, he still prayed his family might change their mind. That putting him in the well was not the answer and they were readying a rope to retrieve him now. But that idea died as the day wore on, as the grey sky faded to black, leaving him in utter darkness. The night sounds echoed down to him as owls flapped overhead, and wolves howled in the distant hills. To his amazement, several fireflies dipped down into the well, settling on random stones to flash their fluorescent bodies in the dark before disappearing back into the world above.

Daniel curled his legs against his chest and laid his head across his arms. His entire body ached with pain and cold, and despite his fear of the dark, he could not stay awake. Before he slipped into sleep, he heard a whisper above him. He snapped his head up so fast, it cracked against a stone behind him and he winced. As he rubbed the growing goose egg, he squinted into the darkness.

"Daniel?"

The voice was unmistakable, and he nearly shouted with joy.

"Ma?"

"Shush, Daniel. You might wake your father."

"Ma, please, don't leave me here. Don't let me die."

"Oh, my darling son. I will never let you die. I can't get you out now, but I'm going to get help as soon as I can. In the meantime..."

Daniel felt the gentle tap of something against the top of his head. He fumbled in the dark to find a cup at the end of a thin rope, filled with bread and cheese.

"Keep the cup to collect rain. If you have to stay down

there a while longer, you won't be able to drink the well water. Try to make the food last until tomorrow night. If I haven't reached help by then, I'll bring you more. Daniel?"

He nibbled on a piece of bread before answering. "Yes, Ma?"

Her soft sobs broke over him, but he didn't call out again. He let her cry as long as she needed.

"I'm so sorry, Daniel. I should have tried to stop this madness sooner."

He couldn't answer her. He wanted to tell her it was all right, that he understood the difficulty of fighting against the power his father exerted over them. But her crying was contagious, and he bent his head to weep into his chest.

"Please, hold on as long as you can. I'm not going to let you die alone in the dark like an animal. I...I love you, son."

"I love you, too," he whispered as he heard the faint swish of her nightdress when she returned to the house.

The evening passed slowly as Daniel shivered in the dropping temperatures. Though summer would arrive soon, the nights remained cold. Eventually his body, exhausted and aching, slipped into a restless slumber. His mind swirled with images of past happiness and the changing seasons of normalcy, before that pastor came to their town.

Sweltering in the summer heat trapped under the tent, Daniel and his family sat in the back row of seats as they listened to the Pastor deliver his tirade. He told them God thought man moved too fast, stopped respecting the old ways, and turned away from Him through modernization.

"Those big city folks, beating their chests over the steam engine and the cotton gin. They don't even know *how* to work the land with their own hands anymore. Their pride and gluttony have doomed us all."

Many of the gathered townsfolk nodded their heads and murmured agreements.

"They call us backwoods rubes, inbred simpletons who would rather brew rotgut whiskey in rusty stills. That as the world moves forward, we'll be left behind to wither away. And to that I say, if joining the modern world means leaving God behind, then I'd rather rot with Him than prosper without Him."

By now the entire congregation had stood, calling out their affirmations of faith. A chorus of "Amen" filled the tent. Daniel stood with them, but could not share in the Pastor's fanatical ramblings. He couldn't tell anyone he wanted to see the inventions and advancements of the outside world, however, not if he wanted to live free from his father's belt or the schoolmarm's switch.

"Those modern men think they know better than God. Can't you see it?" the Pastor continued. "Cholera is sweeping the land, guided by His hand to punish all sinners. People of Rawsonville, will you not join me to defer our Savior's wrath and save your precious souls?"

Before Daniel knew it, his parents raised their hands, shouting hallelujahs along with the majority of the worshipers. The Pastor began to sing, and soon the entire tent filled with the strains of a hymn that Daniel had heard, and sung, many times. But today it took on an ominous tone, and as the final verse ended, the fevered breathing of all the attendees blanketed him with a dark dread.

"Happy the man that keeps my ways; the man that shuns them dies."

By the end of that week, the Pastor had convinced everyone that the bodies of those who had died of any cause other than illness should be moved next to each family's well. That way, the power from the deceased's obvious healing faith, could penetrate the life-giving water everyone needed. It would prevent the further spread of disease, provide extra strength to the living to fortify their own faiths and avoid catastrophe.

Within a month, every family moved their buried dead next to the wells, and plotted spacing for fresh graves as well. The town's panic grew, however, as the spread of cholera didn't slow. Rather, it increased in speed and numbers. The Pastor told them to hold fast, not lose faith, and continue burying their dead near their individual water supplies. They needed trust that Jesus would take the life essence of His passed servants to heal the living.

For six months, the town heeded the Pastor's advice, never once questioning its validity. Cholera spread out of control, showing no signs of slowing, and the people's desperation brought them to worship each week with the hope for release from this torment. As winter set in, the Pastor preached about a new way to save the population.

"Good people, I believe God needs us to do more to save our town. The dead, though helpful, are not enough. We need the living to step up and add to the sacrifices being made."

"What does God want from us, Pastor?"

"Why has Jesus forsaken us?"

"What more can we do?"

The townspeople filled the tent with their lamentations. The Pastor raised his hands, and soon the cries quieted.

"He has not left us to die, dear faithful, but calls on us to do more. Remember, we have to *show* the Lord our faith, practice it every day, in every way, for Him to know we are His loyal servants. And I believe I have the answer."

By that evening, the blood sacrifices began. Small at first, a needle jab here, a cut finger there. Some, like Daniel's parents, struggled with the mutilations. It pained them each time one of their children cried. For others, the bloodletting justified their true vicious natures in a society that had muzzled them too long.

One morning on the way to school, Daniel passed his neighbor, Mr. Rontal, as he dragged his daughter toward the well at the side of their house. Rebecca screamed and pulled, but Mr. Rontal never relented. Though the shrieks of his daughter, and even the fierce determination set in his scowl, didn't scare Daniel the most. The hatchet Mr. Rontal carried in his right hand frightened Daniel into a shocked standstill.

Though he wanted to run—home, school, to anywhere from there—Daniel stood rooted in place as he watched the macabre spectacle unfold before him. By the time the duo reached the well, Mrs. Rontal burst through the door and ran to them, reaching and scrabbling at her husband's grip on Rebecca. She pleaded with him to stop.

"John, you can't do this. You'll kill her!"

Still clutching his daughter, Mr. Rontal pushed the butt of the hatchet against his wife's chest, knocking her to the ground.

"Mary, you know this is the only way to save Junior."

"Papa, please don't."

Mr. Rontal yanked on his daughter's arm, holding her extended hand over the well opening.

"I'll make it quick, baby. Take comfort in knowing this is what will save your brother."

He raised the hatchet overhead, and with one last screech from Rebecca, Mr. Rontal lopped off his daughter's hand. A tendril of freezing dread crawled up Daniel's spine as he heard, even over the cacophony of shrieking and sobbing, the soft splash of Rebecca's dismembered hand when it hit the water.

Mr. Rontal threw the hatchet down. Using both hands, he squeezed his daughter's arm as if wringing out a water-soaked towel. Rebecca sagged against the well. Her skin paled to the color of day old ashes in a fire pit. He released her then threw a wooden bucket down into the water. Using the crank and pulley, he raised the full bucket, and set it on the wall where he released it from a thick rope. Pulling out his daughter's severed hand, Mr. Rontal tossed it back into the well before marching inside the house.

Mrs. Rontal pushed past him and ran to her daughter's unconscious form, cradling her against her breast. The blood flowed from Rebecca's stump as her mother whispered the Lord's Prayer. Daniel fell to his knees. He felt the hot tears burn against his cold cheeks as he wondered how far Rawsonville would fall before this nightmare ended.

As it turned out, farther than he ever could have imagined.

A week after Rebecca bled to death on the Rontal lawn, John Junior recovered from his illness. Whether he had cholera or something less virulent was never openly discussed, but the Pastor latched onto the boy's miraculous recovery as proof they followed a virtuous path. Soon, the town swarmed with both children and adults missing various appendages or limbs, some hiding mutilation scars under various clothing styles, head wraps, or hats. And for those like Rebecca, more folks attended funerals than any other communal event that winter.

As the spread of cholera abated, to much rejoicing from the townsfolk, another disease popped up to join it. Though no one could agree on the exact cause, its symptoms and virility horrified everyone. The more common issues included muscle tremors, slurred speech, violent mood changes, and difficulty moving until the inflicted could no longer walk or eat. Death came slow and tortuous.

Even the great Pastor, with his shouting sermons and righteous indignation pointed at all the sick, couldn't avoid this new "sin". By the first signs of spring, as the fresh green shoots of tulips and daffodils poked through the warming earth, he and several members of his family suffered from the Tremors. It was with this humiliation that the Pastor devised his most gruesome cure of all.

One Sunday, instead of meeting at the large tent set up in the open field outside of town, the Pastor directed everyone to his home. Or at least as many of the town's people that weren't ill or incapacitated. Daniel and his father stood front and center of the crowd as the Pastor grouped them around his well. He held his son in a firm, though shaky, grasp. His wife watched from the porch, her limbs trembling as she struggled to control them. The Pastor stared at those standing before him.

"My flock, my brethren. I bring you here today to reveal God's new plan, that son of a bitch."

The attendees took one collective gasp, and Daniel stared up at his father. Though the rest of the group expressed concern, Daniel's father stood rigid, studying the Pastor as a student would a teacher, waiting on his next lesson. The Pastor wiped his mouth, clutched his son tighter, and continued.

"Good people, that fucker up in Heaven, high in all his glory..."

The Pastor paused to let out a soft giggle, which the townsfolk nervously shared, before continuing.

"God demands more to help rid us of this new scourge. The blood is not enough, though it seemed good enough for his bastard son. But for us, we need more."

"What more can we do, Pastor?" a woman in the crowd cried out.

"That's why I brough you here, you ignorant slut. Behold."

The Pastor faced the well, still holding his son by his shoulders. The boy struggled, trying and failing to free himself. The Pastor pulled his shaking arm back and slammed it forward into his boy's face, knocking him to the ground.

Stunned but not unconscious, the boy squeaked his surprise as the Pastor picked him up and threw him into the well. In seconds, the sound of splashing water echoed around them, followed by several minutes of choking and coughing. The Pastor smiled.

"I proclaim that in one week's time, my wife, that poor creature, will be cured. Next Sunday we shall congregate here, where I will show you fucking proof of it."

Daniel believed the Pastor's unsettled gait and vocal outbursts showed as much disease as his quivering wife, but it was not his place to speak. Especially with the intense gaze his father settled on him at that moment. He put his arm around Daniel's shoulders and squeezed, sending a sudden sharp pain down to his little finger. His father led him home, the others mumbled amongst themselves and left the property, while the screams and cries of the Pastor's son floated on the north wind that still held the icy chill of winter.

That night, Daniel's father explained, to those in the family who couldn't attend the Pastor's service, the new plan going forward. His eyes shone with something Daniel never saw before. As his siblings and mother peppered him with questions, his father stared at Daniel while he explained.

"I am confident this new plan is right for our family, though we should wait to witness the proof, in the unlikely event it doesn't work the way we'd like."

His father's head twitched, a small movement, hardly noticeable to anyone not paying attention. But Daniel saw it. He'd seen it five times before—from his mother and four siblings. Daniel now remained the only healthy person in his family, and one of the few in the entire town. He didn't know if he should be grateful, or terrified.

The following Sunday, the town of Rawsonville gathered at the Pastor's home. Even those near death had been brought by their families, Daniel presumed, so they could witness the miracle of God's cure. Even his ailing mother attended, carrying Maddie in her trembling arms. His father, who had become prone to random bursts of laughter and violent mood swings, bore the twins and his crippled brother in a wheelbarrow. The heavy load dug a deep track through the fresh mud brought on by late-night rain.

As they waited on their redeemer to spring forth from his home, healthy and cured, the steam of their collective breaths swirled around them like a fog before dissipating into the grey sky. After nearly thirty minutes of shivering, brought on as much by the cold morning as by disease, the door to the Pastor's home creaked open.

The gaunt and pale form of their Pastor convulsed against the screen door. It bounced off his body every time the spasms took hold, its squeaky hinges offering a disconcerting rhythm. His round eyes, wide as hawk's eggs, stared above the heads of the crowd. His mouth opened and closed as his jaw moved up and down, though nothing but garbled speech fell out from between his lips.

He stood on his porch, throwing a hand up into the air then screamed nonsensical gibberish, before collapsing forward and sliding face first down the steps. The great Pastor rolled to a stop several feet from his house, where he lay thrashing in agony. His wife stumbled through the door a moment later, her symptoms just as violent, but more controlled. She gave the Pastor a passing glance as she lurched through the side yard, toward the well.

The solemn congregation cleared a path for her as she passed. Stopping at the low wall, she turned to look at the people, her eyes spilling tears, and her mouth twisted into a grimace. She slurred out two words.

"My...son..."

As Daniel watched in horror, she arched her back, as if to stared up at the sky and God Himself, before flinging herself into the well.

No one cried out; no one tried to stop her; no one ran for help. The crowd merely turned away, from the sounds of splashing water, from the grunts emanating from the fallen Pastor, and dispersed. Daniel studied them as they parted ways. Some shook their heads, their dream for a cure defeated. But many glared at the healthy members of the community as they returned to their homes.

The same way that Daniel's father looked at him.

And now Daniel waited. As the sky lightened above him, he heard the back door creak seconds before his mother's face appeared. A few curls of chestnut colored hair hung down, the strands bouncing as she twitched.

"Daniel?"

"Yes, Ma?"

He could hear her sigh of relief.

"I'm going to ask Mr. Harrison if he'll take me to Annarbour with him this morning. It might take all day, but I'm going to put an end to this. Will you be all right?"

"Don't worry about me. But please, hurry before this whole town ends up at the bottom of a well."

She choked back a sob before they reached for each other in unfulfilled comfort, their hands grasping at the empty air between them.

"I love you. I'll be back as soon as I can."

"I love you, too."

Daniel listened to her footsteps as they faded away. He pressed his head against the wall and closed his eyes, trying to calm his pounding heart. It wouldn't be long now. Maybe tonight, or tomorrow morning, his mother would return and get him out of here, as long as he could survive a little longer.

By the beginning of the third day, Daniel feared the worst. The bread was gone, and they'd had little rain the night before, which provided him with enough drinking water to keep him alive another day. When his father came to the well, throwing the heavy bucket down that just missed cracking against Daniel's head, Daniel could hear the rage in his voice.

"Your mother ain't coming back, son. You know that don't you?"

Daniel didn't respond. He pressed his lips together to keep from crying out his denial.

"She left all of us behind," his father said before succumbing to a boisterous fit of laughter. Daniel's tears warmed his face, and he bit into his fist to refrain from playing into his father's madness. He heard the back door slam open and what sounded like a body collapsing into the mud. His father continued to laugh, and Daniel heard the soft, incoherent mumbling of his brother, Francis. He couldn't understand the words, but Daniel realized it didn't matter.

He stared at the rope and thought how easy it would be to end it. Right now. His bones ached with cold, his shoulder still throbbed from the initial fall, and his very soul cried out for release. With a trembling hand, Daniel reached for the rope and pulled himself to standing. While his father raged on with laugher, he released the bucket from the end of the rope and tied a slip knot.

But before he could think to try it, though, he heard something else alongside his father's cackling. A low, rumbling like the sound of approaching horses. Could it be...?

Over the cacophony of hoof beats and wagon wheels, a chorus of shouts filled the air. When the horses stopped, the yells grew louder as fights broke out among the townspeople and the new arrivals. His father laughed and bellowed curses.

"Trespassers. Help, they're invading!"

Daniel stared up at the small circle of sky, wishing he could see who had come. After more scuffling, a lone rifle shot rang out in the morning air, its echo trailing off amid the sudden silence. And while the people stood hushed in shock, Daniel heard the sweet cry of his mother's voice.

"Daniel? Daniel!"

"I'm still here, Ma."

His mother's silhouette, back lit by the morning light, popped into view, and he could hear her smile.

"Daniel, I'm here. Hang on."

She called to someone behind her, and several men peered over the well wall.

"What in the name of God?"

"Are you all right, boy?"

Daniel cried and bent over at the waist, overwhelmed by a rush of relief and pure joy.

"Can you tie the rope around you, son?"

He straightened. "Yes."

Daniel stepped into the loop he'd already made, and let it slip up around his chest. It pulled tight against his shoulder, but he endured the pain as he rose out of the well. The bright sun burned his eyes and he covered them as the men set him on the ground.

"Lord in Heaven, what have you people been doing here?"

Daniel's mother ran to his side and threw her arms around him. Her body twitched and jerked, sending fresh pain into his shoulder, but he didn't care. He pulled her close while she whispered in his ear.

"I'm so sorry, Daniel. I'm so sorry."

Someone tucked a blanket around them both, and they cried in each other's arms while chaos reigned around them.

They buried Daniel's father, as well as anyone who died from cholera or the Tremors, in the cemetery on the outskirts of Rawsonville. The few survivors moved away, never to return. Someone from the local court decided to build a dam in the Huron River, burying Rawsonville under the newly named Belleville Lake, ridding Daniel of any reminder of the living nightmare his community had become.

Daniel, his siblings, and his mother were transferred to the main hospital in Annarbour. Though Daniel recovered from his injuries, the rest of his family succumbed to disease. After the last funeral laid his brother to rest, the hospital transferred Daniel to the Protestant Orphan Asylum in Detroit until he could find a new family.

The next ten years passed quickly for Daniel. Though he still woke screaming from sleep terrors, and suffered panic attacks on a weekly basis, his new family created a loving and patient environment for him to heal. His two adopted brothers and one sister protected him the moment he entered their home. They acted as living shields, always there to provide comfort, kindness, and peace.

By the time Daniel prepared to enter medical school, Nicolas and Donald had already established themselves as successful lawyers. Divia taught English Literature at a local university. He and his adopted family enjoyed the community's respect and admiration on all aspects of life.

On his last night home, Daniel sat at his writing desk in the room he'd shared with his brothers. He checked items off a list to make sure he hadn't forgotten to pack anything essential for school. As he held the fountain pen in hand, hovering over the recent check he'd marked on the paper, his arm began the familiar tremble. The bicep shuddered twice, then cramped. Pain shot up into his shoulder, his old injury burned anew. Soon his left arm did the same, and he struggled to control the spasms.

A snippet of a thought popped into his head. *He could beat this. He didn't have to perish like his family did, like most of Rawsonville had. There was a cure, wasn't there? He was sure of it.*

His muscles jerked again and he accidentally stabbed himself with the nib. A small bead of blood swelled on the tip of his finger and without thinking, he stuck it in his mouth. As the coppery fluid coated his tongue, he felt his eyes go wide with a faraway memory.

Daniel pushed back from his desk with a small tic of his neck muscle, a shoulder twitch, and a smile. He made his way downstairs and into the kitchen. His mother called down as he stood in front of a set of drawers.

"Daniel, what are doing up? You need to get your rest before heading off to university."

"I know, Mother. I'm just getting some warm milk to help me sleep."

"All right, dear. I'll see you in the morning then."

Daniel opened the drawer to his right and stared down at the collection of shining cutlery. He wrapped his hand around the thick handle of a carving knife, its honed edge glinting in the overhead light.

"The morning, yes."

He held up the blade and giggled.

THE DREADFUL SISTERS WHO REMAIN

"I can't say I'm sorry because it would be a lie. And despite the horrors I have visited upon you and the world, I am not, and never will be, a liar."

She offered him a sympathetic smile, her pointed fangs glistening in the wan light. "Everything you have spoken since we met has been a lie, doctor, including your name. I will only recognize your lack of remorse because that is the only truth you carry. And you will die with that truth on your lips."

She accepted the surrender in his stare. Euryale gripped his throat, digging her thick fingers into his soft flesh. With one quick twist, she removed his head from his neck. His body crumpled to the floor and when she dropped the head, it landed on the corpse with a soft squish. Euryale wiped the man's blood on the remnants of rags he'd allowed her for modesty's sake. His comfort, not hers.

Her sister, Stheno, moved next to her, glaring down at the dead human. She clicked her claws together, their sharp ticks echoing through the cold laboratory. She relaxed her wings and folded them against her back.

"Looks like you owe me one, Lee."

Euryale sighed her exasperation. "Sister, please refrain

from speaking my name in such a crude manner, at least when we are alone."

"You got it, *Yer-eye-uh-lee*. But I don't think we're alone."

The soft shuffle of stockinged feet approached the pair. The source belonged to the doctor's unfortunate deceased wife. She moved without purpose, her vacant gaze focusing on nothing and no one as she walked. She spent most of her days in this repetitive stupor, trailing back and forth through the empty rooms of the house.

As she passed the sisters, she turned her gaze fell to husband's lifeless body. For the first time since she woke as a prisoner here, Euryale saw a flicker of emotion scuttle across the woman's face without the assistance of a fresh victim's blood. Her features scrunched together, distorting her expression from nonchalance to agony within seconds.

The woman's mouth gaped and a whisper, like the dying cry of an injured animal, echoed through the room as she threw herself on top of her husband. She clutched his shirt, shook him as if he were sleeping, desperate to wake him.

"It appears a sliver of soul clung to her during her resurrection."

"It's rare but does happen from time to time."

"You have seen such a thing?"

Stheno nodded. "Centuries ago when that madman kidnapped me. His daughter's soul clung to her physical form causing an unbreakable psychosis. He had to destroy her in the end."

"What a waste."

The wife finally noticed the two sisters standing over her. She reached for Stheno, clinging to her thick legs. A ragged whimper escaped her throat begging for help. With no response she turned to Euryale, and recognition widened her eyes.

She grabbed the tattered clothing at Euryale's waist, ripping them further. The wound in her right side glistened, still not completely healed. The wife's arm shot up, scrabbling for the incision, eager to tear it open again.

Scales popping up like gooseflesh, Euryale slapped the woman, who moaned as she fell back. Undeterred, she rose to her knees and lunged forward, the desperation in her eyes bordering on insanity. Euryale grabbed the woman by her long scraggly hair then lifted her off the ground. She thrashed in Euryale's grip.

Raising the woman above her head and whipping her down, like shaking water from a drenched garment, Euryale separated the woman's head from her body. The pop of her spine as it shattered drowned out the rending of flesh and skin and tendons. The wife's body collapsed on top of her husband's and Euryale tossed the detached head atop them both.

Stheno laid a hand on Lee's shoulder.

"Let's get the hell out of here."

"Stheno, please, must you—"

"Fine, fine." She cleared her throat. "And now, sister, let us take our leave of this decrepit dwelling and find respite so you may fully heal and regain your strength."

Euryale smirked. "Thank—"

"AKA, let's blow this popsicle stand!"

Euryale shook her head. "Come, Stef. Let us go home."

"So Ionian planned this all along? Using your blood to bring back his wife?"

Euryale exhaled. "Yes, but his name wasn't Ionian. Just another link in the chain of lies he made to bind me in trust."

Stef chuckled. Euryale glared at her older sister. "What is so amusing?"

"Exactly how old are you, Lee? A centuries old immortal falling for a human's tricks."

"Surely you remember you are older than I. How is it that *you* could not see through his ruse either?"

Stef opened her mouth to reply then quickly snapped it shut. The sisters left the lab and the house behind, walking hand in hand as the setting sun painted the sky orange, red, and purple.

"There are only two left, my dear. Once they've met with justice, we can leave this place and go on with our lives."

Emily could only mewl, a deep saddened keening that Euryale had come to recognize as resignation. Why the doctor couldn't, or wouldn't, acknowledge it could only be explained by the joy he felt at her return.

Or he was insane. By Euryale's standards, anyone who raised the dead back to life was bound to a mindset of fury.

From her shackled nook, Euryale watched the doctor fawn over his dead bride, caressing the flaky skin of her blue cheek, kissing her cracked hands. He pulled a handkerchief from his pocket and wiped the fresh blood from her lips. Emily turned away, as if embarrassed for having bitten the throat from the man lying at their feet. The doctor gently pulled her chin so she would meet his gaze.

"You never have to be sorry for this, my darling. He died that night when he dared to touch you. They all did. It's just that death showed up a little late, that's all."

Emily patted his hand but again looked down at the body, the fresh blood glistening in the fluorescent lights. Though her speech never recovered, after a kill she moved like a regular human, even expressing love for her husband. And yet, within hours, she would return to the shambling, vacant-minded corpse that he'd resurrected a month prior.

The doctor approached Euryale, a shameful half-smile dominating his expression.

"I know I ask a lot of you, Euryale, and I promise it's almost over. But for now, I must take more."

She leaned back against the wall and turned her gaze away from him. "Why do you bother to speak, Doctor? You do as you will, in spite of my protests and threats."

"You understand why, don't you? You see the proof standing before your very eyes. Emily, my dearest Emily, has returned."

"That is not your wife."

"Well, of course she is."

Euryale turned her head to look at him. During her first week of captivity, her mind raged, planning and plotting the doctor's demise the moment she could free herself of these charmed shackles. But as she stared at his gaunt face, studied his shaking hands, and noted the welling of unshed tears in his eyes, she sighed.

"Perhaps this delusion fuels your quest for vengeance, but I have grown weary. Take your dose of blood and leave me be."

She turned away from him again and listened as he fumbled with his implements. She'd stopped showing her fangs and scales to him weeks ago but whenever he cut into her flesh, they showed themselves against her will. The doctor flinched every time, amazed and horrified by her true form. But was never sorry.

"I'm hoping to lure the last two simultaneously so I will need to procure more this time."

The cold steel of the scalpel bit into her flesh. She couldn't help but watch as he gathered her blood into a conical flask instead of a test tube. He filled it to the base of its neck before pressing his handkerchief against the wound. Though unnecessary, Euryale supposed his humanity, such as it was, instinctually tried to help as much as it hurt.

"Ah, yes. This should work. I've been studying the ancient parchments. I'm hoping this amount will give my Emily a more...permanent temperament."

"You cannot be serious."

"I would never lie about such a thing."

Euryale could feel a cruel sneer stretch across her face.

"Doctor, I am confused by two things. One, do you honestly believe your Emily will ever return as she was?"

"Of course, I do. Otherwise, why would I even try?"

Euryale scoffed, an incredulous snicker echoing through the lab. The doctor remained unshaken. Still, he did stop working on his mixture to turn and look at her.

"And what is the second thing that confuses you?"

Euryale stared at him. She could feel the heat rising to her face; scales popped up across her skin like gooseflesh and her fangs emerged.

"Do you honestly believe, doctor, that when this is over, when your revenge is complete, that I will allow either of you to live?"

His already milky skin paled to the color of ash left in an ancient hearth. He adjusted the tie at his neck and cleared his throat. The shaky smile couldn't hide his fear. He turned back to his experiment.

"As long as those shackles hold and the spells remain intact, I'm afraid you can't do anything to harm either of us."

She looked from the metal bindings at her wrists to the scrawled pictograms within the niche.

"I suppose that is true, doctor. But you must have forgotten. Though I am a rare and ancient beast, I am not the only one."

His hand stopped, hovering over the flask as a white

powder fell from his fingertips. His shaking worsened and his bravado slipped.

"We are in a most secret place, I'm afraid. By the time anyone finds it, Emily and I will be gone. So I must implore you to refrain from these vague threats, and let me concentrate."

She sighed again, too tired to engage in such trivialities with this human. He was right in at least one aspect. He had her trapped and powerless against his whims. Unless an outside force worked in her favor, Euryale could do nothing to change her circumstances.

Within minutes, the doctor finished his concoction and stored it in a small refrigerator under one of the lab tables. That same sheepish grin returned as he picked up a clean scalpel and test tube before approaching her left side. She glared at him.

"I thought you wanted to mete out justice in a different fashion, doctor."

His gaze flicked to the left where Emily stood, staring down at the dead man at her feet. The doctor frowned; the only time she'd ever seen him look disgusted. He pressed his fingers against her ribs and plunged the scalpel between two of them. She clenched her jaw to keep her fangs from extending. Immortality didn't make her impervious to pain.

He began to fill the tube with more of her blood, though this fluid held a ribbon of black ooze that swirled with a life of its own.

"Be careful, doctor. Even a drop of that will fell the largest and strongest of men, let alone a coward of the highest echelon."

He jerked the half-filled tube away before quickly placing it in a metal rack. Wiping his dry hand on his smock, he strode over to Emily who already started showing signs of a zombified state. Glancing over his shoulder at Euryale, the doctor escorted his wife out of the laboratory.

"Come, my dear. Let's get you more comfortable and out of this dreadful room. Perhaps some tea on the veranda?"

Emily moaned, allowing him to lead her back into the house. Euryale laughed, a humorless guttural cackle, as the heavy steel door shut her in darkness.

Euryale awoke to a searing pain in her right side. She could feel the warmth of her own blood as it oozed down her flank. The cool metal of various restraints pressed against her body, rendering her immobile. Blinking, she rolled her eyes to the left. The mundane implements of a scientific laboratory filled the fuzzy edges of her vision: two rolling gurneys, multiple low tables covered with medical instruments, and every shape and size of glass and metal beakers filled with various liquids.

The body of a woman on the table beside her, however, struck her as the farthest thing from ordinary she could ever have encountered.

Human, from what Euryale could determine. Long, thin, blonde hair; a smattering of pale freckles marked her cheeks and shoulders. What had likely once been a visage of beauty sunk into darkened eye sockets and rotten flesh. The advanced decay of the body made identification problematic but even if a living woman laid there, Euryale would have no way of knowing her.

She did recognize the man fussing over the corpse. Dr. Ionian crossed Euryale's path no more than seven days ago. He'd impressed her as highly intelligent, passionate, and driven. She hadn't encountered another like him in decades. That plus his name, and the city in which he lived, tugged at her sense of nostalgia and longing for her homeland of Greece.

"Your name is Dr. Ionian and you live in Ionia?"

He chuckled. "People mistakenly believe my family

founded the town when, truth be told, it's the opposite. My ancestors renamed themselves after the town. Apparently, a scandal forced them to flee their previous home, and in order to hide from the pursuing law, they changed the family name."

"How fascinating. What had they done?"

"I'm not familiar with all the particulars. My grandfather was rather tight lipped about the whole ordeal. But it had to do with..."

He paused to look around, as if afraid someone might overhear. He placed his hands on either side of his mouth and whispered, "Medical experimentation."

She stared at him, her eyes wide, and he laughed.

"My wife always got a kick out of the old stories. She'd pretend to be shocked, threaten to tell the town council so they'd come with their pitchforks and torches."

"You should not make light of that. If I have learned nothing else in my life, it is that humans are easily frightened and will destroy anything that makes them feel weak."

"You speak as if you're not part of the human race, too."

She'd nearly forgotten herself during the conversation, but he smiled and continued.

"You are correct. It was just our way of coping with such nasty rumors, which still survive to this day. My Emily's jokes helped soothe the pain."

"You must love her a lot."

"I did. I do. Unfortunately, she's been gone for two years. I must admit I'm still struggling with the loss."

His face flushed a bright pink and he rubbed a roughened hand across his stubbly chin. "Please forgive me. I've prattled on too long about my problems. Tell me about you. What brings you to this small community out in the middle of Nowhere, Michigan?"

That was the beginning of their friendship. Or what

Euryale believed to be friendship. She'd gone too long since bonding with anyone aside from her remaining sister. They'd both understood the power of loss, how death could darken the souls of those left behind. After that human murdered their younger sister, she and Stef had wandered the world, bitter and angry with the human race. They meted out justice against anyone who'd given even the slightest offense.

Eventually, they parted ways, each tired of the other's company and their shared hate. Euryale held that feeing close, letting it warm her through her journeys. But every few centuries, she'd meet a human that showed her another characteristic of its species, one that chose love over fear, hope over despair. Dr. Ionian allowed Euryale a glimpse into that world with each meeting.

This milquetoast man hardly screamed "mad scientist" yet here he sat, claiming a horrific family history worthy of the myths of her youth. Unfortunately for her, lowering her guard, forgetting the duplicitous nature of the human animal, would prove to be her downfall.

"Are you familiar with the Greek poet, Hesiod, and his poems of the Gorgons?"

She blinked, yet again surprised. Not by the fact this man knew of the tales. Nearly every human she encountered knew the stories in one form or another. It was the *way* he asked the question, how his eyebrows raised as he looked at her; how he leaned forward to create the pretense of intimacy. Not until she felt the sharp pain in her thigh did she realize her mistake. Her gasp came out more of a hiss and Dr. Ionian pulled back, still holding the syringe in his left hand. His didn't display malice, only sympathy. He felt sorry for her, an emotion she hated more than any other.

"I am sorry, my dear. I need your help and considering who and what you are, I knew you would deny my request. I promise I won't hurt you. At least no more than might be necessary to complete my experiments."

"You...fool." Her words stuck between her teeth. The drug he'd administered must be powerful indeed to subdue even a Gorgon.

That was her last memory before the present moment, Dr. Ionian bent over a dead woman, and she shackled to this table. It finally dawned on her the corpse was Emily, the doctor's dead wife. Despite the modern marvel of embalming, the grave had not been kind to the woman. Either the doctor's delusion prevented him from noticing, or he simply didn't care. Either way, with Euryale's blood, the rotting corpse would soon be up and mobile.

Gerald sat in the police briefing room, shoulders slumped, his face still wet with tears and his wife's blood. The steaming cup of coffee sat untouched before him. The investigator across the table, a young inexperienced man of no more than twenty years, cleared his throat again.

"Doctor?"

Gerald raised his head and stared at the detective; his brow furrowed in confusion.

"I beg your pardon?"

"I asked if you could give me a description of the men who did this."

"Yes, I'm sorry. I, uh, there were four of them. All appeared around your age, scruffy, like those thugs from the movies about motorcycle gangs."

"I'm afraid there is a lot of gang activity in this area, some kind of rogue motorcycle group. Most of those guys are harmless, just bike enthusiasts, you know what I mean?"

The doctor stared at the detective, and the man rubbed a hand across his cheek.

"No, I suppose you don't. What were you doing in that alley anyway?"

"Are you insinuating this is our fault?"

"Of course not. It's just I—"

"You assume a couple of old fuddy duddies don't understand the 'real world' and just walk around as if life is just a bed of roses."

"That's not what I meant."

"No, you only mean to help, don't you, detective? To what end? We both know you'll never catch them and even if you do, I'm sure there will be little to no evidence of their guilt."

"Please, sir, I'm sorry. If you could just give a statement—"

"Oh, I'll tell you everything. But don't think for one minute that I'll be waiting around for the police to bring those...those *murderers* to justice."

Gerald played the interview over in his head as he sat in his living room. He gave the police the whole story from the short walk from the theater to their car, to the final blow that took Emily's life, and every horrible act in between. He had no faith in the police, in society, or the law to make this wrong right.

But he had faith in himself.

The former warmth and inviting atmosphere of their home lay quiet and hollow. Emily's absence made it less somehow, smaller, insignificant. He stared down at his hands, the palms still raw with scrapes from when the men had first knocked him down. His and Emily's dried blood stiffened the cuffs of his dress shirt.

Emily.

Fresh tears spilled onto his hands, stinging the raw wounds. He clenched his fists, squeezing blood onto the thick pile of the beige carpet. He moved his hands back and forth, creating the shape of a question mark onto the floor. What would he do now? What was his next move? How could he go on without Emily by his side?

Dr. Farrow.

The name popped into his head. An old colleague, Gerald had neither seen nor thought of Farrow in years, not since the man moved to Europe a decade ago. Though they'd gone in different directions academically—he into chemistry and Farrow anthropology—they'd always remained close friends, each trying to outdo the other comparing the difficulties of their fields.

Surely Farrow would have an answer. Studying dozens of culture's histories, politics, mythologies, and rituals, Farrow must have come across information that could help Gerald with what he had in mind.

Part of him recognized, if only for the briefest of moments, that he'd cracked from grief. What he was even considering, let alone already beginning to plan, would assure him a one-way admittance into Walter Reuther Psych. He didn't care. Life without Emily would be unbearable. He had to do *something*.

Within a month, Gerald sat in Farrow's home as they sipped tea and stared out at the deep blue water below. Farrow stared at his friend over the delicate China cup, his bushy eyebrows raised in shock.

"You can't be serious."

"Oh I most assuredly am, my friend."

"Resurrection."

"Yes."

"Emily's resurrection."

"Naturally."

"And you've come to me because...?"

Gerald stared at his friend. Farrow's lips curled up into a lopsided grin.

"All right, yes. I've encountered many a belief and custom across multiple cultures when it comes to black magic."

"I'm not talking magic, Farrow. That implies make-believe."

"Fine, fine. I understand what you're getting at. But you don't honestly believe any of them can be real, do you?"

"I do, and I intend to prove it."

Farrow sighed and put his cup on the table. "Look, Gerald. I understand what you're going through."

"No, you don't."

"Touché. Even so, this is not the path for you to follow. It's not real."

"It is. It has to be. I'll find it but I need your help."

"I won't do it. I will not help you literally dive headfirst into this black pool of madness, Gerald."

Farrow pushed his chair back from the table and turned to walk away from the conversation. Gerald lurched forward, grabbing his friend by the arm.

"You have to help me, Richard. You have to."

Gerald fell to his knees, weeping and sobbing like a child.

"I beg you. You have to help me find it. You think I've gone mad. I haven't. But I surely will if I have to live one more second, drowning in the hopelessness that has threatened to overcome me since the moment Emily took her last breath."

Farrow stood over his longtime friend. His heart broke with Gerald's every cry, every hitch that rocked his body. He knelt down and laid a hand on the man's shoulder.

"All right, my friend. All right. I'll help you. God forgive me, I'll help you."

Two years of dusty libraries, archeological digs, historical site visits, eating questionable dishes, and draining half his savings to "get in good with the locals" just to find any small snippet of information on resurrection rites. But eventually it paid off. Musty books, ancient carvings, oral histories, and more all contained the same nugget of information regarding one ingredient key to every ritual he'd found: Gorgon blood.

Euryale and Stheno sat at a small table at an outdoor cafe. The week of scorching temperatures had broken after a heavy rainstorm. The cool damp air reminded them both of the summers they'd lived back home in Greece, centuries before.

"Who knew Podunk, Michigan would have such a similar climate to Corfu."

"Stheno, why must you speak with such vulgarities?"

"It's Stef now. And you gotta get with the times. We walk around talking the way you do—"

"You mean properly?"

"Like you've got a giant two by four jammed up your ass, and people will start looking at you funny. And when people start doing that, they notice how different you are."

Euryale nodded. "And when they notice those differences, they get scared."

"And out come the pitchforks."

"I know, I do. It is just so distasteful."

"I know we haven't seen each other in decades but we're together again. I'll help ease you into the 21st century as painlessly as possible. Whaddya say?"

"I suppose I have little choice in the matter."

"Exactly. And no better time like the present. That guy over there has been staring at you for the past ten minutes."

Euryale turned to look but Stef gripped her arm.

"Don't look, Lee. We don't want to be obvious."

"Oh, in the name of Anthena's little owl. Please do not call me—"

"Damn, he's coming over. Act natural."

"Is that not the precise opposite of what you want me to do?"

"Shush."

"Excuse me, ladies. I'm sorry to interrupt."

Stef smiled at him. "No sorry necessary. What can we do for you?"

The man nodded at Stef but turned his full attention to Euryale.

"May I sit?"

Euryale looked up at the human. Small in stature, middle aged or older, someone she could snap easily in two if necessary. Not a threat.

"If you must."

"Lee," Stef hissed at her sister. She covered the faux pas with a laugh and gestured for the man to take her seat.

"Please, sit. I was just leaving anyway."

"Where are you going?" Euryale clenched her jaw to refrain from showing panic. Though this human may be of little concern, she didn't need to display *any* weakness in front of him.

"Don't worry about me, Lee. Please, enjoy..."

"Oh, uh Ionian. Dr. Harvey Ionian."

"Enjoy *Doctor* Ionian's company for a while. I'll call you later."

"Call me what?"

Stef waved goodbye and practically skipped down the sidewalk. She glanced over her shoulder at Euryale, offering a wink and a wave, before disappearing around the nearest corner. Euryale wanted to run after her but the man cleared his throat and she turned her attention back to him.

"Are you sure I'm not interrupting?" he asked.

"You will have to forgive her, doctor. She and I do not share the same ideas when it comes to societal niceties."

His mouth split into a wide grin and to her surprise, Euryale found herself mirroring his expression.

"Why do you smile so?"

"Forgive me. I'm not laughing at you or anything so rude. I just haven't heard anyone speak so well since my wife passed. So many youngsters today with their slang and mutilated grammar."

"Oh, if only my sister had remained. It would be good for her to hear such words. She is like a nagging elder the way she scolds me about my speech."

The doctor's eye widened in surprise and he coughed. "Your sister?"

Euryale nodded. "Older one at that. Sometimes she acts younger than her years."

"Ah, yes. My older brother used to be the same way. Always called me an old fuddy duddy, even in our youth."

They shared a laugh and Euryale realized she enjoyed Ionian's company. She hadn't opened herself up to any interactions with humans for decades. Perhaps building a new friendship would be good for her, one she could enjoy for years to come.

ABOUT THE AUTHOR

Peggy Christie is an author of horror and dark fiction. Her horror fiction/art collaboration with Don England, Plague of Man: SS of the Dead, can be found through Amazon; multiple short story collections, as well as her novel, Primordial, from Dragons Roost Press; and her vampire novel, The Vessel, from Splatter Theater Press. Peggy is one of the founding members of the Great Lakes Association of Horror Writers, as well as a contributing writer for the websites of Cinema Head Cheese and Malevolent Dark. Check out her webpage at themonkeyisin.com for more information on her other publications and appearances.

Peggy loves Korean dramas, dogs, survival horror video games, and chocolate (not necessarily in that order) and lives in Michigan with her husband and their dog, Willow.

facebook.com/authorpeggychristie

instagram.com/pmonkey710

amazon.com/Peggy-Christie/e/B00P8IZK4U

Primordial

After being unemployed for too long, Charlie lands a job at a local advertising agency. Once there, she accepts a position on the Secretarial Council, only to find that the secretaries don't answer to human laws and ethics. They worship an interdimensional creature, who stumbled into our world eons ago, to get everything they want through sex, fear, and death.

Now Charlie must figure out how to stop this creature from wreaking havoc and chaos throughout humanity before it's too late.

Dark Doorways

Enter this dark mansion of ghastly delights. Each dark doorway opens to another tale of horror. Some rooms are large banquet halls, others are tiny servant's quarters. Each contains wondrous, fear inducing words from master scribe Peggy Christie. If you have the courage, take hold of one of the latches, open the door......and enter.

Hell Hath No Fury

Ever wonder how you might handle a sabbatical from work? Think the bible told you everything there is to know about the Devil? What if the noises coming from under your child's bed weren't just in his imagination? Crack open Hell Hath No Fury, a collection of 23 tales of horror and dark fiction, to learn the answers to these questions.

DRAGON'S ROOST PRESS

Dragon's Roost Press is the fever dream brainchild of dark speculative fiction author Michael Cieslak. Since 2014, their goal has been to find the best speculative fiction authors and share their work with the public. For more information about Dragon's Roost Press and their publications, please visit:
http://www.thedragonsroost.biz

www.ingramcontent.com/pod-product-compliance
Lightning Source LLC
Chambersburg PA
CBHW060641260626
47161CB00008B/2948